BETWEEN TWO WORLDS

When Peace Is Just A Different Kind Of War
A Story of Unbroken Resilience

Andrew Rose

ZFD Books

Little Elm, Texas

DEDICATION

To my wife:

I want to thank you. In writing this novel, I faced the revelation that deep-seated trauma had created a fortress of protection around me - one I couldn't even see. Only through these pages did I realize that throughout our marriage, I revealed only a small part of myself, hiding the rest to protect us both from further harm.

In the years since you honored me with your hand, you have navigated an emotional rollercoaster that only you had the strength to endure. It will be a lifetime mission, but I dedicate the rest of my days to stripping away that fortress, finding a way into the light, and navigating the complex future that lies before us.

If you can find it in your heart, take my hand one more time. Let us truly stand side by side to face the world and whatever trials the future holds. Because in the end, it is us against the world, and we have the two most precious reasons to fight: the walking, running chaos on legs that are our boys. With the grace and strength of Jesus Christ powering us, and our little Angel baby looking over us, there is nothing in this world that can destroy us.

To my boys

To my Angel son

I might not think of you every single second of every day, and for that, I am sorry. But please understand, that does not mean my heart doesn't ache every time I am reminded that I never got to hold you. I know you are with our Lord and Savior, shining down and cheering us on. In my dreams, I hear your laughter, and in my heart, I rejoice that you were spared this cruel and unforgiving world. For reasons unknown, God chose you to be ours, but pulled you back. I pray that the lesson was learned so this wasn't in vain. I know one day I will look into your eyes and tell you how much I love you. Until then, know you are missed, and you are thought of.

To my oldest

From the day you were born, you changed my life in ways I never imagined. When I held you in that OR, and your eyelids struggled to open to look straight into mine, you did something no one else on earth could do: You took down my defenses. For the first time, my mission was not to protect myself, but to protect you. I might not show it all the time, but you are the reason I strive to be a better man than I was the day before. I know I fall short of that "Best Dad Ever" title, but I try with all my might to earn it, and I hope you see that. The pride I feel for the young man you are becoming is beyond words. The joy you bring to my soul is the fuel I use to push forward.

To my youngest

You are the chaos on crazy I never knew I needed. Your fearless spirit teaches me every day that obstacles do not matter. If you lower your head and barrel through, eventually you will get past them. In your short life, you have been through so much, yet you find laughter every day. No matter how many stitches you get, you puff out your chest, stand tall, and declare, "Mine." Your confidence inspires me to face my challenges head-on and never cower in fear.

To both of you

I love you beyond what words can explain. Do not let this ugly world take anything from you. Remember that *you* determine the path you take. No matter what you choose, choose to be a light. Choose to strengthen those around you. Live a life of service and dedication.

Remember that words are cheap, but actions speak volumes. Remember that knowledge is power, but money often corrupts. Remember that family consists of people who show you mutual love and respect, not just those who share your DNA. Remember that when someone wrongs you, it speaks to their character, not yours.

Walk through this world unapologetically doing good, even if you are looked down upon for it. Titles, status, celebrity - these are distractions. While they look shiny on the surface, just below is rot and ruin. Find a path to peace, love, and compassion. That is where you will find satisfaction.

Remember that real men protect, no matter the cost. A real man doesn't need to proclaim he is the "alpha." A real man watches. He observes. A real man learns, participates, and is present. A real man sharpens his tools and keeps them oiled, but he also washes the dishes and folds the laundry. A real man doesn't hesitate to go to the store to buy pads for the women he loves. A real man understands that his outward appearance might portray domestication, all while he prepares for the moment he might need to be the warrior. It is better for people to say, "I didn't know he was capable of that," than to say, "I thought he would have been able to handle it."

Take these words. Make them your own. Find the flaws and keep the sound. And one day, when you are sitting in front of a screen typing words to your own kids, remember me for a split second. Know how much I loved you. Know that I did my best.

To the cast of my past

To all the others in my life story - thank you for your part in making me the person I am today. Whether you inflicted the trauma, ignored the signs, or watched from the sidelines doing what you thought was best, I wouldn't be this driven to speak out against the ugly in this world without you. I cherish the trauma I endured because I hope my story helps at least one other person realize that the stigma placed on victims is further abuse. We should not be ashamed. We should not hide until our abusers die. We should proudly say: I survived, and here I stand. I stand to shine a light on the predators and expose their evil. I am stronger because I survived.

To the silent warriors

To all the veterans and non-veterans struggling with mental health: You are stronger because you are making it. We should not hide our battles to make the world comfortable in the lie that we are alone. The truth is, everyone is suffering to some degree. If enough of us choose to put down the mask and stand side by side, the illusion of isolation will disappear.

It doesn't just take a village to raise a child. In a world governed by selfishness and greed, it takes a village to stand strong for the good and the moral. It takes a village to stand arm in arm and proclaim: "I will not be victimized anymore. I will not be silenced anymore. I will tell my story."

Because in the end, **Your Story Matters.**

PROLOGUE
THE BELL

October 2004 - Salah ad Din Province, Iraq

The desert doesn't care about your plans. It doesn't care that Santos and his squad have survived the meat grinders of Samarra or the perimeter of Fallujah. It doesn't care that we are months away from going home. It just waits.

We were driving back into the sunrise. That's the golden hour in Iraq - when the dust suspended in the air catches the light and turns the whole world into a soft, hazy painting. It's deceptive. It makes you feel like the danger has passed with the darkness. We were coming off a three-day mission, a high-value target raid deep in the desert that had gone perfectly. No shots fired. We bagged the guy and his security detail while they slept. It felt like a victory lap. We were invincible. We were the "unscathed" platoon.

We were close to Highway 1. Maybe two hundred meters from the pavement that would take us back to the FOB, back to the showers, back to the phone center where I could call home.

"Hey, you want the turret?"

It was a casual question. A toss-up. Usually, I was the gunner - the eyes of the truck, standing tall in the hatch, gripping the .50 cal. It was the position of power, but it was also the position of exposure. The wind, the dust, the noise.

Akin, my teammate in the lead truck's shadow, wanted a turn.

"Yeah, go for it," I said.

I slid into the back seat behind the driver. It was a downgrade in view but an upgrade in comfort. The hum of the diesel engine was a steady vibration against my spine. I did something I rarely did outside the wire. I unclipped my chinstrap and took my helmet off. I rested my head against the thick, multi-layered ballistic glass of the window. The glass was cool, or at least cooler than the air outside. I closed my eyes for a second, letting the rhythm of the convoy lull me.

I didn't hear the explosion. You never hear the one that gets you.

I felt it.

It hit my chest first - a massive, invisible hammer swinging through the armor of the truck, compressing my lungs before my brain could register the threat. Then the world tilted violently. The truck rocked on its suspension, a ten-thousand-pound beast kicked by a giant.

My head, still resting against the window, slammed into the ballistic glass.

The lights went out.

It wasn't black; it was a swirling, violent kaleidoscope. Stars burst behind my eyelids. And then came the bells. A high-pitched, screaming ring that drowned out everything else. I opened my eyes, but the world was a silent movie. I could see the chaos, but I couldn't hear it. I saw the gunner's legs bracing in the turret. I saw the dust, now thick and choking, filling the cab.

I looked out the window - the same window that had just tried to crack my skull. The truck in front of us was engulfed in black smoke. We weren't stopping. We were accelerating.

Push through. Get out of the kill zone.

I felt the collision before I understood it. Our bumper slammed into the rear of the burning truck ahead of us. We were pushing them, shoving the disabled vehicle out of the blast radius. I could feel the heavy *thump-thump-thump* of the .50 cal firing above me. I couldn't hear the shots, but I could feel the percussion vibrating through the chassis, shaking my teeth.

Ambush.

The word floated up through the concussion fog. My training kicked in, overriding the short-circuit in my brain. Door open. Weapon up. Move.

I stumbled out of the truck into the blinding light. The air tasted of sulfur and burning rubber. We were taking small arms fire, but to me, it was just puffs of dust kicking up around my boots. The silence was terrifying.

My squad was moving toward a field on the right side of the road. It wasn't open desert; it was a dense, agricultural nightmare. Crops, tall grass, maybe six or seven feet high, creating a blind maze. I followed Sgt. Graves, stepping into the green.

The engagement was visceral and close. I saw a figure running - a weapon in his hand. We opened up. Suppressive fire cut through the stalks, shredding the vegetation. We pushed forward, hunting ghosts in the grass. We found them. Three enemy KIA. One of them was still clutching a plastic cell phone detonator.

A piece of plastic. That's all it took. A cheap piece of plastic to shatter the morning.

"Clear!" someone yelled. I could hear it now, faintly, as if they were shouting from underwater. The bells were still ringing, but the world was leaking back in.

We moved back to the road. The dust was swirling again, this time from the rotors of a Blackhawk medevac. It was already lifting off, banking hard against the sun. I watched it go, feeling a strange detachment. I walked up to Sgt. Graves.

"Who was it?" I asked. My voice sounded strange in my own head. "Who was in the lead truck?"

He looked at me, his face caked in dust and sweat. He said the name.

"It was Akin."

It wasn't just a name. It was my friend. The guy I joked with. The guy who was going home in a few months.

I looked at the black scorch mark on the road. I looked at the heavy glass of my window, where my head had hit. I touched my temple. Survival wasn't a skill. It was a seating chart. It was a casual conversation. It was a switch.

The "unscathed" platoon was gone. We were just like everyone else now. Broken.

CHAPTER 1

THE LOTTERY

1984 - Puerto Rico

The ringing stopped, but the noise didn't. The dry, metallic silence of the desert was replaced instantly by a wall of sound so thick you could lean against it. It was the sound of a thousand frogs screaming in the night, the coquí calling out from the wet darkness. It was the sound of chickens scratching at hard-packed dirt, roosters crowing at hours that made no sense, and the frantic, rapid-fire Spanish of adults fighting for their lives.

Santos was four years old, and the world was made of knees.

He stood in the center of a sweltering town hall meeting, surrounded by a sea of legs clad in polyester and denim. The air didn't taste like sulfur and burning rubber here; it tasted of stale sweat, cheap cologne, and the heavy, suffocating humidity of the tropics. This wasn't the kind of heat that baked you dry like a kiln; this was the kind that wrapped around you like a wet wool blanket and squeezed.

His mother's hand was a vice around his wrist. She was gripping him so hard his fingers were turning numb, but he didn't pull away. He knew better. Even at four, Santos understood the barometer of his mother's moods. Today, the needle was buried in the red.

She was vibrating with energy - a frantic, jagged electricity that made the people around her step back slightly. To a stranger, she looked like a young woman determined to secure a future for her son. To Santos, she felt like a grenade with the pin pulled halfway out. The Traumatic Brain Injury she had suffered as a child was invisible to the crowd, but it was the governing law of Santos's life. It left her with the emotional regulation of a pre-teen and the strength of a grown woman. She didn't negotiate; she exploded.

"Stay close," she hissed, yanking him out of the path of a sweating man waving a piece of paper.

The room was a madhouse. It was a lottery, a bidding war, a desperate scramble for the most basic human necessity: a roof. The government was handing out *parcelas* - plots of land with small, pre-fabricated structures. To the officials at the front of the room, it was urban planning. To the hundreds of families shouting and pushing in the hall, it was life or death.

Santos watched the chaos with wide, dark eyes. He didn't understand the economics of poverty yet. He didn't know that they had moved from the Bronx to this island to live with grandparents, or that they were currently suspended in a fragile web of family charity that was rapidly fraying. He just knew that everyone wanted a key, and there weren't enough keys.

Suddenly, a voice boomed over the localized shouting. A name was called.

His mother shrieked. It wasn't a scream of fear, but of victory. She dragged Santos forward, cutting through the crowd like an icebreaker. She snatched the paperwork from the official's hand before he could even offer it.

They had won.

The prize was located in a "village" of identical structures, set up in a grid on the edge of the wilderness. Santos stood in front of their new home, staring up at it.

It was a tin-roofed box.

It was no bigger than a small camper trailer, a single room with a kitchenette in the corner and a space for a bed. The walls were thin; the roof was a sheet of corrugated metal that magnified the sound of the rain into a deafening roar. It was a shelter, yes. It was a place to sleep.

But as Santos walked inside, shrinking into the corner as his mother paced the twelve-foot span of the floor, he realized something else. In the Bronx, or at his grandparents' house, there were other rooms. There were doors to close. There were closets to hide in when the yelling started.

Here, there was nowhere to go. The *parcela* was intimate. It forced them together. There was no separation between his mother's volatility and his own skin. If she was angry, he was in the blast radius. If she was manic, he was the audience.

Outside, the village was alive. Kids ran shirtless through the dirt streets, chasing stray dogs and cats. Neighbors shouted greetings and insults across the narrow gaps between the houses. It looked like freedom. But inside, with the door shut and the tropical sun heating the tin roof until the air shimmered, it felt like a cage.

And he was locked in with the tiger.

Life in the *parcela* was governed by two things: the sun and the mood.

The sun was the clock. The shack didn't have insulation; it was essentially a solar oven. By 7:00 AM, the corrugated metal roof would start to pop and groan as the metal expanded in the tropical heat. It was a rhythmic pinging sound, like someone tapping a spoon against a pot, that served as Santos's alarm clock.

Waking up meant peeling himself off the mattress. The air inside was thick, smelling of stale sleep and the kerosene stove.

Breakfast was a lesson in government economics. Santos sat at the small, wobbling table while his mother prepared the meal. It wasn't eggs and bacon. It was the "Bloque." A massive, rectangular block of bright orange government cheese that came in a cardboard box, accompanied by a bag of rice and beans paid for with *cupones* (food stamps).

She sliced the cheese with surgical precision. Even in poverty, she had standards. She fried it in a pan until the edges were crispy and brown. It was salty, greasy, and filling. It was the fuel of the poor.

But the peaceful clinking of forks on plates was fragile. The TBI lived in the gaps between seconds. One moment, his mother was humming, flipping the cheese. The next, disaster struck.

Santos knocked over his cup.

It was a plastic cup filled with water. It wasn't juice. It wasn't milk. It was just water. It spilled across the vinyl tablecloth, dripping onto the dirt floor.

In a normal house, this is a "clean it up" moment. In the *parcela*, it was a declaration of war.

His mother froze. The humming stopped. She turned slowly, her eyes wide, the pupils dilated. The switch had flipped. The adult woman vanished, replaced by the impulsive, unregulated child trapped in her brain.

"Look what you did!" she shrieked. The sound was too big for the small room. It bounced off the metal walls, magnifying the rage. "You are clumsy! You are stupid! You ruin everything!"

She grabbed the rag and slammed it onto the table, scrubbing the water violently, as if the water were acid burning through the table. She wasn't just cleaning a spill; she was fighting a chaotic universe that refused to stay in order.

Santos shrank into his chair. He pulled his knees up, making himself small. He didn't argue. He didn't cry. He engaged the stealth mode that would later serve him in the orchards of Iraq. Be still. Be silent. Wait for the threat to pass.

And just as quickly as it started, it ended.

The water was gone. She threw the rag into the sink. She took a breath. The tension left her shoulders. She turned back to the stove, flipped a piece of cheese onto his plate, and smiled.

"Eat, papito," she said, her voice sweet, as if the last sixty seconds hadn't happened.

She didn't remember the rage. But Santos did.

He ate quickly, shoving the hot cheese into his mouth, burning his tongue. He needed to get out. He needed to escape the blast radius before the wind changed again.

He pushed his chair back and slipped out the front door.

Outside, the village was already awake. The heat was oppressive, but at least it was open. Chickens pecked at the hard-packed dirt. A mangy dog slept in the shadow of a banana tree. Neighbors were shouting greetings across the fences - loud, boisterous laughter that sounded like fighting but was just conversation.

Santos walked to the edge of their plot. He looked back at the tin box. It looked sturdy. It looked like a home. But he knew the truth. It was a pressure cooker, and he was the steam.

If the tin shack was the storm, his grandparents' house was the anchor.

It was only a short walk away in the *parcela*, but crossing their threshold felt like entering a different country. The air didn't vibrate with tension here. It smelled of *sofrito* - the holy trinity of garlic, peppers, and cilantro frying in oil - and strong *café con leche*.

Abuela was the heart of the operation. She was a woman of motion, always stirring, sweeping, or folding. She didn't speak the language of rage; she spoke the language of food. When Santos arrived, usually escaping the aftermath of a spilled cup or a "bad mood," she didn't ask questions. She just pointed to a chair and placed a plate in front of him.

Arroz con gandules. Stewed chicken. A slice of avocado.

"Eat," she would say. It wasn't a command like his mother's; it was an offering.

Abuelo was the silence. He sat on the porch in an old, creaking wicker chair, a man carved out of the island's history. He didn't say much, but his presence was a heavy, protective blanket. When he was there, the monsters stayed away.

He carried a folding knife in his pocket at all times. In the Bronx, a knife in a pocket meant danger. Here, it meant dessert.

It was for the mangos and the avocados that grew heavy in the yard.

They would sit there as the sun went down, the heat of the day radiating off the concrete. *Abuelo* would pull out a mango, the skin blushing red and orange, and flick the knife open. With hands that were rough like sandpaper but gentle as a surgeon's, he would slice the fruit.

He would cut a slice and pass it to Santos, the juice sticky on his thumb.

"Uno pa ti," he would say softly. One for you.

He would cut the next slice and eat it himself. "Uno pa mi." One for me.

They would eat in rhythm with the *coquí* frogs starting their evening chorus. *Uno pa ti. Uno pa mi.*

It was a hypnotic, peaceful cadence.

But then, the twinkle would hit his eye. He would cut the next slice, hold it out to Santos, and just as the boy reached for it, *Abuelo* would pull it back and pop it into his own mouth.

"Dos pa mi!" he would laugh, his chest rumbling. Two for me!

It was a simple joke, repeated a hundred times, but Santos laughed every single time like it was the first. He would laugh until there were tears in his eyes, not from the humor, but from the sheer relief of it.

They would sit there for hours, enjoying the sticky sweetness of the fruit and the sound of the wind in the trees. They were enjoying the peace. They were enjoying the "nothing."

For a few hours, Santos wasn't a caregiver. He wasn't a target. He was just a grandson sitting in a wicker chair, safe in a world where the only surprise was who got the next slice of mango.

It was perfect.

But the sun always went down. The shadows would stretch across the dirt road, reaching out like fingers to drag him back.

"You should go home," *Abuela* would say gently, handing him a container of leftovers for his mother. "She will be worrying."

She wouldn't be worrying. She would be waiting.

Walking back down the dirt path, the knot in Santos's stomach would retie itself. He could see the outline of his own tin shack against the purple sky. It looked dark. It looked hungry.

He held the leftovers tight against his chest, a small shield against whatever version of his mother was waiting for him behind that metal door. He stepped off the road and into the shadows, not knowing that this fragile balance - the cheese, the tantrums, the grandparents down the road - was about to burn to the ground.

CHAPTER 2
THE FIRE

1985 - The Parcela

The cage didn't stay empty for long.

Santos learned early that a vacuum in his mother's life was always filled by chaos. This time, the chaos had a name, a heavy step, and a smell that soured the air in the tiny shack.

The boyfriend moved in, and the walls of the *parcela* seemed to shrink.

In a house the size of a rich man's closet, there are no secrets. Violence isn't an event; it's an atmosphere. It hung over the kitchenette where beans boiled; it hovered over the bed where they slept.

Santos became a ghost in his own home, mastering the art of stillness. If he was quiet enough, if he pressed himself hard enough into the corner, maybe the anger wouldn't find him.

But the *parcela* was too small for hide-and-seek.

The memory of the violence wasn't linear; it was a series of flashbulbs popping in the dark. A hand striking flesh. The sound of a body hitting the thin metal wall, making the whole structure shudder like a drum.

One night, the target shifted. The boyfriend's rage spilled over, and Santos wasn't quick enough to vanish.

He felt hands on him - not the gripping hand of his mother, but hands that wanted to hurt. He was lifted, weightless for a terrifying second, and then thrown.

He hit the far wall of the shack, sliding down to the dirt floor, the breath knocked out of his small chest. He didn't fight back. He just sat there and cried, a high, thin sound that was swallowed by the tin roof.

But his mother heard it.

The TBI that kept her mind in a perpetual pre-teen state also stripped away the brakes on her rage. Seeing her son thrown like a ragdoll flipped a switch.

She didn't scream. She grabbed a hammer.

The violence that followed was fast and ugly. It was the frantic, clumsy violence of survival. The hammer connected. Then, she reached for the machete kept near the door for cutting brush. It wasn't a warning; it was a retaliation. She stabbed him.

The police arrived in a swirl of lights that cut through the village darkness.

To a five-year-old watching from the floor, they should have been the heroes. They were the men who restored order.

They handcuffed the bleeding boyfriend. They looked at the blood on the floor, at the dented wall, at the small boy with wide, wet eyes.

Then, one of the officers turned to Santos's mother. He didn't offer comfort. He didn't offer a victim's advocate.

"Next time," the officer said, his voice bored, "don't let him out of the house. Finish the job."

It was a lesson Santos would never forget: The law wasn't there to save you. It was just there to clean up the mess.

The timeline blurred after that. The boyfriend was taken away - to the hospital, then to jail. The shack was quiet for a time. But the quiet didn't last. He came back.

It was during this period - after the stabbing but before the end - that the strangest memory occurred. It was a memory of trapped motion.

Santos was in the back seat of a car at night. The vinyl seat stuck to his legs. His mother was in the passenger seat. The boyfriend - the man she had stabbed, the man who had thrown Santos - was driving.

The air in the car was thick, heavy with unspoken things. They weren't going home. They were driving up into the mountains, into the deep, pitch-black darkness outside of town.

They stopped at a bar. It was late, far too late for a child to be awake.

The boyfriend got out, but Santos stayed in the darkness of the backseat, watching the shadows of the mountains.

He remembered the feeling of confusion - why were they here? Why was she with him? The fear wasn't acute; it was a low-level hum. He just wanted to go home. He wanted to be back in the *parcela*, even if it was a cage.

At least it was *their* cage.

But the cycle was winding tighter.

Not long after that night, the final warning came. Perhaps the boyfriend had been picked up again, or perhaps the threats had simply become too loud to ignore. The police - the same force that had told her to kill him - reached out with a message:

He is getting out. He is coming back.

This time, the tone was different. It wasn't advice; it was an alarm.

They didn't wait. His mother grabbed Santos, grabbed a few bags, and fled. They ran to his grandparents' house in Ceiba, putting miles of road between them and the tin box.

The *parcela* was left behind. But it wasn't empty. The dogs and the cats - the strays his mother collected and fed - were still inside.

The news came the next morning. The Fire Chief stood in his grandparents' living room, his face grim, holding a hat in his hands.

"It's gone," he said. "All of it."

But it wasn't just a fire. It was an execution.

The Chief explained what they found. When the fire crews arrived, the structure was fully engulfed, a torch lighting up the village grid. They tried to make entry, thinking the woman and the boy might be inside. They hit the door. It wouldn't budge. They went to the windows. They wouldn't open.

The boyfriend hadn't just set a fire. He had brought chains. He had chained the doors from the outside.

He had taken nails and hammered the windows shut. He had sealed the *parcela* into a tomb before striking the match.

He wanted them trapped. He wanted them to burn alive.

"We couldn't get in," the Chief said. "By the time we broke through, there was nothing to save."

The drive back to the *parcela* felt like a funeral procession.

It was the day after the fire. The sun was high and cruel, illuminating everything that the darkness had hidden the night before.

Santos sat in the back of his grandfather's car, clutching his seatbelt. He didn't want to go back. He wanted to stay in the safety of the *sofrito* smells and the concrete porch.

But his mother needed to see it. She needed to know it was real.

They parked on the road. The air didn't smell like a neighborhood anymore. It smelled like a wet campfire - that cloying, heavy scent of soaked charcoal and melted plastic.

Santos stepped out of the car.

The silence was the first thing that hit him. The *parcela* was usually noisy - chickens, dogs, radios. Now, it was dead quiet.

He walked toward the plot. The devastation was absolute. The tin sheets of the roof were twisted into tortured shapes, like crumpled paper. The wooden frame was gone, reduced to black skeletons lying in the mud.

But it was the details that made his stomach turn.

He saw the door frame. It was charred black, but the heavy steel chain was still there, fused to the wood by the heat. It was wrapped tight, looped through the handles and secured with a padlock.

He stared at it. *He locked us in.*

It wasn't just a fire. It was a cage. If the police hadn't warned them, if they hadn't run to the grandparents, Santos would have been waking up to the smell of smoke, running to the door, and pulling on a handle that wouldn't move.

He would have pounded on that wood while the heat rose. He would have died scratching at the exit.

He looked away from the door and down at the ash pile.

Small, black shapes were scattered in the debris. The stray dogs. The cats. The animals his mother had fed and cared for. They hadn't escaped.

They had been trapped inside the perimeter, confused and terrified as the world burned around them.

A wave of nausea rolled over him. *That's me,* he thought. *That's us.*

His mother stood beside him, weeping silently. She wasn't crying for the clothes or the mattress. She was crying because she saw the chains too. She realized how close the "Final Warning" had been to a death sentence.

Santos stepped back. His sneaker sank into the wet gray sludge of ash and water. He looked up at the sky where the roof used to be.

The officer's voice echoed in his head, louder than his mother's crying. *"Next time, finish the job."*

The boyfriend had tried to finish his job. He had brought chains. He had brought nails.

Santos wiped his nose with the back of his hand. He didn't cry for the dogs. He locked the image of the chain in his mind - a permanent file in the cabinet of his trauma.

He realized then that survival wasn't about being good. It wasn't about being safe. It was about being gone before the lock clicked shut.

After the fire, the world didn't end. It just got smaller and safer.

They moved into his grandparents' house in Ceiba. It wasn't just a place to sleep; it was a fortress.

For a long while - time was a blur to a five-year-old - life actually felt good. The threat was gone. The boyfriend hadn't just disappeared into the night; the law had actually worked for once. He was captured shortly after the fire, charged and convicted of arson and attempted murder.

He was in a cage of his own making, and the key was thrown away.

With the monster gone, the fear evaporated.

Santos slept in a small room with his mother. It was cramped, but it was safe. There were no footsteps to listen for. There were no curtains catching fire.

During the days, the *parcela* poverty felt miles away.

His grandfather was a mechanic of necessity - he fixed things until they couldn't be fixed, and then he fixed them again. Santos became his shadow. He would stand next to him in the driveway, handing him wrenches while he leaned under the hood of a car.

They didn't talk much. They listened to a small, battered AM/FM radio that crackled with salsa and local news.

Click, clack, hiss. The sounds of the ratchet and the radio were the soundtrack of peace.

When he wasn't fixing cars, he was in the jungle. The neighbors had lush backyards that spilled over with green. They climbed mango trees, shaking the branches until the fruit fell with heavy thuds. They ate them right there, sticky juice running down their chins, laughing with friends who didn't know or care that his house had burned down.

He was just a kid. He thought this was it. He thought they had landed.

But the restless energy that defined his mother's life couldn't sit still in the quiet of Ceiba. The peace was too loud for her.

"We are going to New York," she announced one day.

It wasn't a debate. It was a directive.

They packed the bags they had acquired since the fire. They said goodbye to the mango trees and the AM/FM radio. They got on a plane, leaving the warmth of the island for the grey concrete of the city.

They landed in New York and moved into his Aunt's apartment.

It was a shock to the system. The apartment was crowded, loud, and smelled of different cooking and different stress. The open sky of Puerto Rico was replaced by brick walls and fire escapes. The freedom of the backyard was replaced by the strict rules of being a guest in someone else's home.

Santos looked out the window at the busy street below, missing the grease under his fingernails and the sound of the *coquis*.

He didn't know it then, but the "Safe Harbor" was officially closed. They were about to enter the system.

CHAPTER 3
THE LINE-UP

1986 - The Bronx, New York

They left the ashes in Puerto Rico, but the smoke followed them to the Bronx.

The move back to New York wasn't a homecoming; it was a retreat. Santos and his mother landed on his aunt's doorstep, refugees from their own life.

For a brief moment, it felt like safety. There were walls that didn't shake in the wind. There was a door that locked properly.

But the expiration date on family hospitality is invisible, and you can feel it when it arrives.

They had been staying at his aunt's apartment for a few weeks. It was a typical Bronx walk-up - narrow hallways that smelled of boiled cabbage and floor wax. Santos slept on the couch, folding up his blanket every morning to "erase" his existence. But the tension was atmospheric.

They were eating their food. They were using their hot water. They were taking up their air.

His uncle finally drew the line. "You have to go," he said.

"We are leaving," his mother whispered to him. "To the city. They will give us a house."

She made it sound like a prize. They packed their bags.

His aunt slipped a twenty-dollar bill into his mother's hand - a severance package for family.

They didn't go to a house. They went to The Intake.

It was a massive, drab building in the South Bronx. They waited for hours in a river of desperation. When they finally sat in the orange plastic chairs, Santos felt the shift. He wasn't Santos anymore.

He was a Case Number.

"Name?" the woman behind the glass asked.

"Rosado," his mother said. "Me and my son. We have nowhere to go."

The woman typed. *Click-clack-click.* She stamped a form.

"Placement," she said. "Emergency Shelter."

They didn't know it then, but they were entering a system with levels. And they were starting at the bottom.

Level 1: The Meat Grinder

The shelter wasn't a home; it was a warehouse for humans.

It was a massive open space, likely a converted drill hall or gymnasium. There were no walls. There were no rooms. There were just rows of green canvas cots separated by a few feet of air.

This was the "Open Shelter" life.

There was zero privacy. You slept with your shoes on and your bag strapped to your chest because if you didn't, it would be gone by morning.

The noise was a constant, low-frequency roar - coughing, snoring, muttering, the squeak of springs.

Every evening, they were assigned a cot. Santos would sit on the edge of the canvas, pulling out a toy or two, trying to carve out a microscopic world of play in the middle of the chaos.

But the worst part wasn't the sleeping. It was the showers.

They were communal, gym-style showers separated only by a small wall and a flimsy curtain. Because he was small, he had to go with his mother into the women's side.

It was a terrifying, confusing parade of flesh. Women walked freely, naked, stripped of their modesty by the system.

To a six-year-old boy, it was overwhelming. But it wasn't just visual; it was interactive.

He remembered women smiling at him. At the time, he thought they were being playful. He thought it was kindness. Looking back, he realized it was a mocking condescension.

One woman, water dripping down her body, jiggled her breasts at him. Another thrust her hips in his direction, laughing.

"Papi," she cooed, her voice sharp with amusement. "You like what you see?"

He shrank back against his mother's leg, confused by the aggression masked as a joke. He didn't have the words for it then, but he felt the violation. In the shelter, you weren't a child. You were just another set of eyes.

The routine was brutal. At 8:00 AM, everyone was evicted. It didn't matter if it was raining or snowing. The guards kicked you out, and the cycle reset. His mother would drop him at school, maintaining the facade, and then walk the streets until evening.

Dinner came in white Styrofoam containers. It was always the same - some form of gray slop with a side of slop. He could still hear the squeak of the plastic fork against the Styrofoam, the sound of a thousand people eating food that tasted like despair.

To get back in, you had to line up. One evening in that line, the crowd surged.

He was playing with a "Can of Worms" toy, holding it to his face. A man shoved him. The metal rim slammed into his eye.

In the common area, they set up a TV at night for movies. Santos would sneak away from his mother's bunk, drawn to the glowing screen like a moth.

The movie playing was *A Nightmare on Elm Street*.

Other kids might have been terrified. A man with a burned face and knives for fingers hunting children in their sleep should have been the stuff of trauma.

But Santos sat there, mesmerized.

Maybe it was because Freddy Krueger was a monster you could see. He had rules. He lived in dreams. In Santos's real life, the monsters were unpredictable - a boyfriend with a machete, a fire that burned pets, a lottery for a tin roof, a line that determined if you slept indoors.

Freddy was scary, but he was fiction. And for ninety minutes, sitting on the linoleum floor with a bruised eye, Santos wasn't the homeless kid waiting for a bed. He was just a spectator in someone else's nightmare. And that was a relief.

Level 2: The Sanctuary

By Christmas, they graduated.

They were moved to a second-stage shelter. It was still a large space, but the energy was different. It was quieter. Warmer.

They were assigned a permanent section - a partitioned area with a twin-sized bed and a little storage box. It felt huge. They didn't have to carry their lives on their backs every morning. They didn't get evicted at dawn.

This shelter seemed to be exclusively for single mothers and children. The aggressive, chaotic energy of the men in the open shelter was gone. The atmosphere was almost church-like - hushed, respectful, safe.

He remembered feeling the tension in his shoulders drop. The "Spidey Sense" - that constant, humming radar for danger - finally turned off.

On Christmas Eve, a Santa came. He handed out gifts wrapped in bright paper. It wasn't about the toy inside; it was about the dignity of being remembered. For a few weeks, they weren't just statistics. They were a family down on their luck, resting in a safe harbor.

But here is the strange thing about that winter: He didn't remember the rest.

He could describe the smell of the burning *parcela* in 4K resolution. He could describe the exact shade of purple around his eye from the Can of Worms. He could recall the smell of the bleach in the Intake Center.

His brain kept impeccable records of the pain, cataloging every threat for future reference.

But the comfort? The kindness? It was a blank tape.

Aside from the flashbulb memory of that Christmas, the rest of their time in the Sanctuary was gone. It was a gray fog.

He thought it was a survival mechanism. Even at six years old, his brain knew that "Safety" was an anomaly. It was a glitch in the system. To fully accept the comfort - to memorize the feeling of a soft mattress or the sound of a quiet room - would have been dangerous.

If he let himself get used to the warmth, the inevitable return to the cold would have been unbearable.

So, he repressed it.

His mind treated kindness like junk data - unnecessary for survival in a hostile world. It deleted the files of peace as soon as they were created. It was a pre-emptive strike against heartbreak.

If you don't remember how good it felt to be safe, you won't miss it when the safety is ripped away.

He sat in that warm, quiet partition, safe for the first time in years, and his brain was already busy forgetting it, preparing him for the next war.

Level 3: The Key

Then came the meeting.

They sat in a small office with a social worker. She looked tired, but she was smiling.

"We have a placement," she said. "You are now on the Section 8 waiting list for an apartment. Until then, we are moving you to a hotel shelter."

They packed their storage box. They took a van to Manhattan.

The Prince George Hotel.

It wasn't the Plaza. Walking in, it felt like a bootlegged version of the Stanley Hotel from *The Shining* - faded grandeur, musty carpets that smelled of decades of cigarettes, and dim, flickering lights in the long hallways.

But then, they got to the room.

They walked in. To the left was a small bathroom. To the right was a chair, a TV, and a window that looked out onto the city.

There was a bed.

But Santos didn't care about the TV. He didn't care about the window.

He turned around and looked at the main door.

It was heavy wood. It had a knob. And above the knob, it had a deadbolt.

He watched his mother close it. *Click*. Then she turned the deadbolt. *Thud*.

He stared at that lock. It was the most beautiful thing he had ever seen.

This space was theirs. The world couldn't shove him here. The women couldn't mock him here. The fire couldn't find him here.

They were still in the system. They were still poor. But for the first time since the *parcela* burned, they were behind a locked door.

He stared at the deadbolt. It was a heavy piece of steel, a mechanical promise of safety.

But as the silence of the room settled around them, the old instinct - the one forged in fire and open floors - whispered a question he wasn't ready to answer.

Had he finally locked the dangers of the past out? Or had he just locked himself inside the lion's den?

CHAPTER 4
THE TROJAN HORSE

1987 - The Prince George Hotel, Manhattan

The Prince George Hotel was a fortress.

To the rest of New York, it was a blight. It was a "Welfare Hotel," a grand, decaying dame of 28th Street where the city warehoused its broken pieces. The lobby was a cavern of faded glory, with peeling gold paint and marble floors scuffed by thousands of desperate boots. The hallways smelled of stale cigarettes and boiled cabbage. The elevators were coffins that smelled of urine.

But to seven-year-old Santos, Room 402 was a castle.

It had a bathroom with a tub. It had a kitchenette. It had a window that looked out onto the gray teeth of the Manhattan skyline.

Most importantly, it had a door with a deadbolt.

For the first few months, life was quiet. The "Spidey Sense" that had been buzzing since the *parcela* fire finally began to quiet down. Santos went to school. He came home. He watched cartoons. He played with his toys on a carpet that wasn't moving.

The "Charity Kid" began to dream of normal things. Maybe this was it. Maybe they had made it.

But deep down Santos knew. As with anything that brought him joy, this too would not last.

1988 - New York City

The predator didn't break down the door. He walked in through a gap in the legal system.

The meeting happened in a courthouse, a place designed for endings, not beginnings. Santos was eight years old, sitting on a hard wooden bench next to his mother. They were there for child support, another bureaucratic hurdle in the obstacle course of poverty.

Then, a man walked in.

He didn't look like the monsters from the movies. He didn't look like the boyfriend with the machete. He looked normal. He looked steady.

His mother stood up. There was a conversation, low and murmuring, that Santos couldn't quite catch. Then she turned to him. She didn't stand in front of him to block the view. She stepped aside.

"This is your father," she said.

Santos looked at the stranger. For years, "Father" had been a blank space, a missing puzzle piece that made the picture of his life incomplete. Now, here was the piece.

Then came the question that would haunt Santos for decades.

His mother, the gatekeeper of his safety, looked down at her eight-year-old son and handed him the keys to the gate.

"It's your choice," she said. "Do you want to have a relationship with him?"

It was a staggering abdication of duty. She placed the weight of an adult decision on the shoulders of a child who was starving for connection.

To Santos, it wasn't a choice; it was a lifeline. He nodded.

After the courthouse, there was a phone call. Then a visit. And with the visit came the gifts. For a boy living in the scarcity of the shelter system and government housing, these objects were magical artifacts.

The grooming didn't start with a touch; it started with a tape deck.

The Golden Age

For a while, the man was everything Santos had imagined a father should be.

He was the "Cool Dad." He didn't bring discipline; he brought gifts. He filled the room with noise and energy.

He brought a color TV to replace the small black-and-white one. He brought brand-name sneakers - Nikes that made Santos feel like a king on the playground, erasing the stigma of the "shelter kid" shoes. He brought food - real food, not the shelter slop. Pizza. Chinese takeout in white boxes. Soda.

The tape deck radio was sleek, modern, and expensive. It was a status symbol. It sang a seductive song: *He can provide things she can't. He has resources. He is safe.*

The gifts bought access. They bought trust. They smoothed over the strangeness of a man who had been absent for eight years suddenly wanting to be present for everything.

Santos was starved for male attention. He soaked it up like dry earth soaking up rain. He wanted to believe. He wanted to be the son who played catch, the son who had a dad to protect him from the bullies at school.

The father knew this. He was a master architect of trust. He built a pedestal and placed himself on top of it.

The erosion of boundaries was slow, a tide creeping up the beach inch by inch.

The Public Secret

The erosion of boundaries wasn't always done in the dark. Sometimes, it happened under the bright fluorescent lights of a kitchen, with an audience of smiling adults.

It was a Friday evening. The apartment was full - his mother, his father, his father's male partner, and two women who were friends of the family. The air was thick with cigarette smoke and the smell of cheap wine.

Santos sat at the kitchen table, a prop in their social gathering, quietly eating while the adults laughed and gossiped.

One of the women, a loud lady with bright red lipstick, leaned over and pinched his cheek.

"Look at them," she cooed, looking at his father. "It is so great to see you two building a good father-son relationship. He looks just like you."

Santos sat up a little straighter. He didn't know what to say, but the praise felt good. He was doing it right. He was being the "Good Son."

His father smiled, taking a drag of his cigarette. He looked at Santos, then at the women.

"Yeah," he said, his voice casual. "We are close. We are lovers."

The air left the room.

Heads turned. The women froze, their wine glasses halfway to their mouths. His mother stopped mid-nod.

The word hung in the air, heavy and radioactive. *Lovers.*

Even at eight years old, Santos knew the word didn't sound right. He knew it didn't belong in a sentence about a father and a son.

He squirmed in his seat, looking at the floor, waiting for someone to yell. He waited for his mother to say, "Don't say that." He waited for the partner to say, "That's sick."

But his father didn't flinch. He leaned forward, sensing the shift in the atmosphere, and smoothed it over with the confidence of a con man.

"You know," he explained, waving his hand dismissively. "Lovers confide in each other. Lovers trust each other. We trust each other, right, Pa?"

He looked at Santos. The room looked at Santos.

The definition was twisted, a linguistic knot designed to trap him.

If he said no, he was saying he didn't trust him. If he said yes, he was agreeing to the label.

"Uh, yeah. I guess," Santos mumbled.

He braced himself for the outrage.

It never came.

The tension broke. The women laughed. "Oh, you are crazy!" one of them said, swatting his arm playfully.

His mother smiled, taking a sip of her drink, accepting the explanation. They nodded. They laughed. They went back to their gossip.

Santos sat there, frozen. The adults - the people who wrote the dictionary of his world - had just edited the definition. They had stamped their approval on it.

If they all agree, he thought, looking at his mother's relaxed face, *then I must be his lover.*

That was the night the safety net didn't just break; it dissolved. His father had tested the waters in public, showing everyone exactly who he was, and they had laughed. He knew then that he could do anything. No one was watching. No one cared.

It was subtle at first. A look. A touch that lingered too long. A game that felt wrong but was framed as "just between us men."

The man used the gifts as leverage. *I bought you those sneakers. I bought you that TV. Don't you love me? Don't you want to be a good son?*

It started in the bathroom.

During visits to his father's apartment, hygiene became a ritual. "Go take a bath," his father would say. It seemed like care. But then the door would open. At first, his father would just sit in the room.

Then, he started getting into the tub.

"It's normal," the silence seemed to say. "This is what fathers and sons do."

At first, his father wore a swimsuit - a speedo that felt uncomfortably revealing but technically covered. Santos sat in the water, knees pulled to his chest, confused but compliant. Then, the swimsuit disappeared.

The nudity became total. The boundary was erased completely, washed away in the warm water while his mother sat in the other room, fully aware, doing nothing.

Santos felt the old "Spidey Sense" flickering back to life. The hair on his arms would stand up when the man entered the room.

But the ultimate betrayal wasn't physical; it was psychological.

It happened on a weekend visit. His father's partner - the man he lived with - was out of town. It was just the three of them: Santos, his mother, and his father.

They sat him down. The atmosphere was serious, heavy with the pretense of maturity. They wanted to have a "talk."

"We need to explain something to you," his father said. "I am gay."

To an eight-year-old, the word was abstract. They explained it in terms of love - some men love women, some men love men. That part was understandable. But they didn't stop at the definition. They decided that a verbal explanation wasn't enough.

"We want you to understand," his mother said.

They turned on the TV. They put in a tape.

It wasn't a documentary. It was pornography.

Santos sat between his parents, bathed in the flickering blue light of the screen, watching graphic sexual acts between men. He looked at his mother, waiting for her to cover his eyes, waiting for her to shout, to turn it off, to be the "keeper" his aunt had tried to be.

She watched the screen. She nodded as his father pointed things out, framing the smut as "education."

In that moment, the safety of the world fractured. The person who was supposed to protect him was collaborating with the person who was corrupting him.

They were a team. And he was the experiment.

The "Charity Kid" knew how to survive hunger and cold. He knew how to dodge a physical blow. But he had no defense against this. This was a Trojan Horse, rolled into his life disguised as a father, and his mother had helped open the hatch.

CHAPTER 5
THE GLASS SHARD

1994 - New York City

The Trojan Horse didn't just enter the gates; he waited for the previous occupant to leave them open.

Before the father moved in, there was "The Husband." He was a tall, quiet Haitian man who had drifted into Santos's mother's life like a low-pressure system.

For a brief, confusing window of time, the apartment had felt almost normal. They got married - a quick, bureaucratic affair that seemed more like a business transaction than a romance.

And it was.

Santos watched him with the wary skepticism of a street dog. He noticed things his mother missed. He saw how "The Husband" checked the mail every day, hunting for one specific envelope. The envelope finally came.

The Green Card.

The transformation was instant. The quiet, steady man evaporated. He found a woman with deeper pockets and packed his bags. The abandonment broke Santos's mother, confirming her deepest fear: that she was useful only as a stepping stone.

The apartment was empty again. The vacuum was created.

But before the permanent move-in, there was the long drift.

During the years that passed between the so-called "educational" video and the first actual physical assault, life was a confusing mix of normalcy sprinkled with strategic conditioning.

The gap consisted of weekend visits, once a month or so. In those early years, the bathing ritual continued - odd, invasive, but stopping short of the unthinkable.

His age was a temporary shield; he was too young for the darker appetites, but just old enough for the mind games.

The grooming shifted from tapes to conversation. He weaponized Santos's interests against his instincts.

He loved Michael Jackson, so he used the King of Pop as a precedent.

"Michael hosts kids at his house all the time," he would say casually. "They all sleep in his bed. It's normal. It's what people who care about each other do."

He was normalizing the bed long before he climbed into it.

And then there were the kisses. They didn't land on the cheek, where a father's kiss belongs. They landed on the lips. They didn't linger - just a quick, dry peck - but the contact left a residue. It put a cold, heavy nausea in the pit of his stomach, a physical signal that his brain tried to ignore but his body couldn't forget.

Then, the line went dead.

After the incident with the video, there was a break. For nearly a year, the visits stopped. Perhaps he realized he had pushed too hard too fast, or perhaps life just took him elsewhere.

But when the phone rang again, Santos was pushing ten years old.

We fell back into a routine, but the rules of engagement had shifted. The bathing ritual stopped.

"You're big enough to shower by yourself," he said. It was a small mercy, a boundary redrawn.

But he found a new way to bind him. He didn't use water; he used silicon.

He had a Personal Computer. To a kid living in the analog poverty of the shelter system, that beige tower was absolute magic. It was a portal.

They would sit side-by-side, not watching TV, but dismantling the machine. They took apart PC towers, exposing the green motherboards and the ribbon cables that looked like city highways. He taught him how they worked. He showed him how to troubleshoot.

For a boy who already loved science - who spent hours looking up at the clouds for meteorology or staring at the stars for astronomy - this was oxygen. It was a natural extension of his curiosity.

It was the most confusing part of the abuse. In the bathroom, he was a predator. But at the desk, with a screwdriver in hand, he was a teacher. He sparked a massive interest in computer science that would stick with Santos for the rest of his life.

He gave him the keys to the future, even while he was locking the door to his safety.

The computer wasn't just for taking apart; it was for connecting.

When they upgraded to a modem, the screeching, static symphony of the dial-up connection became the soundtrack of his evenings. *America Online.* It was a gateway to the outside world, and for a pre-teen boy, that meant one thing above all else: Girls.

His interest in them was blooming. It was a normal, healthy curiosity - the biological directive of a boy becoming a young man. He wanted to talk to them. He wanted to see them.

His father saw this interest. He didn't discourage it. He didn't give him the "respect women" talk. Instead, he saw another lever he could pull. He saw a way to take his normal development and twist it to serve his own warped reality.

He would sit next to him at the desk, the glow of the CRT monitor lighting up their faces.

"You like girls, right?" he would ask. It sounded like a buddy cop movie. It sounded like bonding.

Then he would take the mouse.

"Let me show you something," he'd say.

He used the anonymity of the internet to bypass the boundaries of the real world. The pictures took a lifetime to download. Line by line, as if the women were pulling down their shirts.

First the cleavage, then the jackpot. "Boobs," the Charity Kid chuckled to himself.

Then came the pressure. His shorts tightening, he shifted in his seat but his father reassured him. "It's perfectly natural, son. Want to download the next one?"

He framed it as education. He framed it as "what men do." But it wasn't education. It was desensitization. He was using his own natural desires as a Trojan Horse to normalize his own deviance. By blurring the lines on the screen, he was trying to blur the lines in the room.

He made him an accomplice in his voyeurism, ensuring that if he ever tried to speak out, he would feel just as guilty.

The images on the screen were just the kindling. His father knew exactly what he was doing; he was lighting a fire in a boy who was just beginning to understand his own body.

The exposure led to a natural progression of self-exploration. He was about twelve years old when he first understood the mechanics of release.

His father, ever the observer, seemed to know this shift had happened.

It culminated during a car ride. We were driving to his mother's apartment. His partner was behind the wheel, eyes fixed on the road. His father turned the conversation to "The Talk."

It wasn't a talk about safety or respect; it was an interrogation disguised as guidance. As the discussion progressed, he maneuvered Santos into admitting that he had experienced ejaculation.

His partner might have been driving the car, but morally, he was asleep at the wheel. He didn't intervene to stop the conversation. To Santos, that silence was a signature on a permission slip - a stamp of approval that allowed the uncomfortable interrogation to continue unchecked.

Seizing on this momentum, his father decided he wasn't going home. He announced he was going to stay a few days at his mother's apartment.

The cot was set up in the corner of his room.

Outside, the city provided the soundtrack to the urban decay - dealers holding down corners, the distant pops of gunfire, and the wail of sirens rushing weary officers to scenes of devastation.

But inside, under the cover of darkness, the real drama was about to begin. The stage was prepared. The audience was asleep.

The scene was set. Three, Two, One. *ACTION!*

As Santos drifted slowly toward the edge of sleep, the sense of danger was already settling into his bones. The sanctuary of the night was compromised. The safety of the Sandman was broken, replaced by the waiting predator in the corner.

The guise of education evaporated. There was no lecture this time, only a question whispered in the dark, cutting through the silence.

"Has any girl ever given you a BJ?" he whispered.

"What? Um, no!" Santos replied instinctively. His defense mechanisms flared, trying to push the question away before he even understood it.

But then came the fatal flaw. The curiosity that he had been cultivating - the same curiosity that took apart computers and looked at the stars - betrayed him.

Curiosity overrode self-preservation.

"What is that?" he asked.

As quick as an auto-reply email, his response came, specific, targeted, and preplanned.

"It's just like a kiss, you know, down there. It's how you show someone you love you want them to feel good."

Santos lay there for a minute, sadness creeping in. "I guess I do not have friends that love me like that," he whispered.

His reply came like a surgical strike, punching deep into the bunker where he was hiding. The impact destroyed everything within.

"I love you like that," he said. "I can show you. I can make you feel good."

It wasn't a question. It wasn't a request. It was a command disguised as affection. It was the prerequisite statement - the twisted permission slip he gave himself before the act began.

The darkness was complete, overwhelming.

In that black void, Santos was drowning in confusion and nausea. He felt the shift in the room, the movement of fabric. His shorts slipped down, and he felt a mouth on him. Comprehension was non-existent.

The darkness enveloped him completely - no sight, no face of a grown man, just the immense, terrifying contradiction of feelings. His brain was screaming *no*, but his biology was confused.

The assault was over in a moment. He would be surprised if even a minute had passed.

His shorts were pulled up. No words were exchanged.

He lay in his bed, numb, a hollow shell of the boy who had gone to sleep just an hour before. The questions raced through his mind, louder than the silence in the room.

What just happened? Why did my body react that way? If this is love, why do I feel so disgusting?

His eyes were wide open, staring into the blackness. But the darkness he was looking at wasn't just the absence of light in the room anymore. He was staring into the darkness that had just taken residence in his soul.

The Occupation

For Santos, this was the beginning of the descent. It was a spiral into social, emotional, and academic self-destruction.

While the outward assault on his physical body was conducted by the man called his father, a second front opened up inside his own mind. Like a twisted pincer movement, Santos began a blitzkrieg assault inwardly.

He attacked himself with shame, with silence, and with a hatred for the body that had betrayed him. The stage for total domination and the hostile occupation of who Santos once was had been set.

The Charity Kid was gone. The Soldier was not yet born.

Now the final battle for what remained was about to begin. Months turned to years. The war persisted.

It was a dark serendipity. Just as Santos's mother was abandoned by her husband, Santos's father was dumped by his long-term domestic partner. He arrived with his luggage and his liquor, pitching it as a family reunion. But Santos knew the truth.

He needed a roof, and she needed a man - any man - to fill the space.

They weren't "lovers" in the romantic sense; they were two broken people using each other for survival and occasional, loveless friction. The apartment became a minefield. The air smelled perpetually of stale beer and impending violence.

The abuse had evolved from the grooming of the "educational" tapes into a daily routine of dominance.

It started with the slaps. It was a casual cruelty - a sharp smack to the back of the head for any infraction, real or imagined. If Santos spoke too loudly, *smack*. If he dropped a fork, *smack*. It was conditioning.

Santos learned to tuck his chin and hunch his shoulders. But the days were just the prelude to the nights.

The sleeping arrangements were the trap. The apartment was small, so Santos's father slept in Santos's room. He had a small bed set up in the corner, separated from Santos's bed by a few feet of floor.

The darkness should have been a wall, but for the father, it was a door.

Santos would lay in his own bed, feigning sleep, his body rigid. He would hear the rustle of sheets from the corner. The sound of feet hitting the floor. The heavy, alcohol-tinged breathing moving closer.

The intrusion wasn't accidental; it was a migration. His father would cross the room and climb into Santos's bed.

It wasn't just shame that kept Santos paralyzed; it was a specific, horrifying fear. A threat had been planted in his mind, a seed of terror that bloomed in the dark.

If you fight, if you pull away too hard, I will bite it off.

The fear of mutilation turned Santos into a statue. He would lie there, tears leaking silently into the pillow, waiting for the act to end, waiting for his father to climb back into his own small bed so the room could return back to the comfort of existential darkness.

Until the night the darkness cracked.

His father had been drinking heavily - a dark, aggressive drunk. The slaps had been frequent that evening. Now, in the dark, the weight was back on the mattress.

Santos felt the familiar intrusion. The disgust rose up in his throat like bile. He tried to pull away, a gentle shifting of hips to signal *no*.

His father didn't stop. He held on tighter, his grip bruising. The fear of the bite flashed in Santos's mind, but something else rose up to meet it. The memory of the *parcela* - where a different man had thrown him - was distant, but the lesson was rising to the surface: *No one is coming to save you.*

Santos didn't think; he reacted. He planted his hands against the mattress and pushed with everything he had.

His father swatted at him, a clumsy, drunken blow meant to subdue.

And the boy decided to hurt him back.

Santos swung. It wasn't a tactical punch; it was a flailing haymaker of fourteen years of repressed anger. His fist connected with his father's jaw.

The physics of the moment took over. His father, off-balance from the alcohol and the surprise, stumbled backward off Santos's bed. He caught his heel on the frame of his own cot and flailed backward.

His head cracked against the wooden window sill with a sickening thud.

But his head wasn't the only thing damaged. Somehow, in the chaos of the moment, the cheap dresser mirror propped against the wall shattered.

CRASH.

Shards of glass exploded across the floor, reflecting the moonlight in a dozen broken pieces. The room fell silent, save for the groaning of the man on the floor clutching his head.

Then the door flew open. His mother rushed in, eyes wide, scanning the scene.

She saw her son on the bed, fists clenched. She saw the father of her child slumped on the floor amidst a sea of broken mirror glass.

"What is going on?" she screamed.

In that split second, the old fear returned. Santos looked at his mother - the woman who had sat next to him during the porn, the woman who had introduced him in the courthouse. He knew he couldn't tell her the truth. In the warped logic of their house, he believed he would be the one in trouble for the sexual act.

So he told the partial truth.

"He hit me," Santos said, his voice trembling. "So I hit him back."

He waited for her to rush to him. He waited for her to check if he was okay.

Instead, she crossed the room, stepping over the glass. She raised her hand.

Smack.

The blow stung his cheek, hotter than any slap his father had given him.

"How dare you?" she yelled. "You do not disobey your father! You do not hit him!"

She knelt by the man on the floor, checking his head, offering the comfort she had never offered him.

He stood there in a state of violent emotional conflict. The initial surge of strength he had felt - the adrenaline of finally standing up for himself - instantly curdled into fear.

As the sting on his cheek began to throb, he wasn't looking at her eyes; he was watching her hands. He wondered if the slap was the conclusion or, like more times than not, just the opening bell of a full-on assault.

He braced himself, his muscles twitching, ready to drop into the fetal position in the corner or on his bed to protect his head and torso from the blows of her fists or whatever object she decided to pick up.

Seconds ticked by. The second blow didn't come.

Realizing the physical assault had concluded, he stood there listening to the berating words pouring out of her mouth. He had stopped listening to the meaning of them long ago. It was always the same set of words.

Whether due to the TBI and her mental limitations, or just because those were her "go-to" verbal weapons she knew were effective, he didn't know. But it was always the same combination of degrading insults, shuffled around to fit the situation.

The usual glaze washed over his eyes as he processed the new data installing itself into his brain.

Standing up for myself only leads to further conflict.

He looked at her kneeling on the floor, tending to the man who had abused him. He now understood.

The only person he could rely on was himself. At that age, he didn't have the tools just yet to fully protect himself, but it was at this moment that his philosophy shifted.

He was alone in this world. Depending on others for protection would only lead to disappointment. Depending on others for love would only lead to conflict.

The sting on his cheek burned, a physical manifestation of the betrayal.

He looked away from his mother, away from the groaning man on the floor, and stared at the wreckage of the mirror scattered across the wood grains.

He saw himself in the jagged shards. His reflection was fractured, split into a dozen different pieces, none of them whole.

Subconsciously, staring at the broken glass, he understood that the shattered reflection staring back at him would stay with him for the rest of his life.

CHAPTER 6

THE INVESTOR

1994 - Far Rockaway, Queens

High School was supposed to be a fresh start.

His mother had enrolled him in a school in Far Rockaway, Queens. It was a hell of a commute from the Bronx - a daily odyssey of trains and buses that took hours - but the distance was the point. It put a physical barrier between Santos and the suffocating reality of the apartment.

For the first time in years, the "Charity Kid" mask slipped a little.

It started with a summer program for incoming freshmen. That summer was a revelation. He found something he hadn't realized he was starving for: A Tribe.

They were a motley crew of outer-borough kids, but they fit together.

Since he was commuting from the Bronx, the school paired him with a girl named Maria in a "buddy system" for safety. They met at a designated subway stop every morning and rode home together every evening.

At first, it was logistics. Then, it was friendship. Eventually, in the quiet, rattling intimacy of the A-train, it became something more. Maria became his first girlfriend. She was his first experience with the possibility of love - a soft, terrifying hope that maybe he wasn't too damaged to be wanted.

Their group was solid. They stood up for each other. They laughed. And despite the fact that his clothes were obvious hand-me-downs and his pockets were empty, they never looked down on him.

Their "leader" - let's call him Edwin - was the glue.

He lived near the school and came from a family that, by their standards, was rich. Every morning, without fanfare or charity, he would slide a tray onto their cafeteria table: Hash browns. McMuffins. Hot chocolates.

To the rest of the world, it was ten dollars of McDonald's. To them, it was a feast. He wasn't buying their loyalty; he was just feeding his people.

In the unwritten laws of teenage hierarchy, that made him King.

Santos was happy to be a knight. He had his girl. Edwin had his. The jock of their group had football. The other two girls were happy to be part of the ensemble cast.

For a few glorious months, they were living in a TV show where the good guys won and breakfast was free.

The Shift

But this was New York in the 90s. The TV show was about to get cancelled.

Around the second semester, the atmosphere changed. Edwin's older brother had joined a known Hispanic gang. To get inroads into the high school, the brother enlisted Edwin to start a "chapter."

It wasn't sold to them as a gang. It was pitched as a "Neighborhood Watch" - an organization for Hispanics to protect each other from the other crews running the halls: The "Red Dragons" (Asian) and the "OGs" (Black).

"We need to look out for our own," Edwin said. It sounded noble. It sounded like brotherhood.

They joined. They wore the colors. They walked with a new swagger.

They hadn't done anything criminal - they were still the kids eating McMuffins - but in the ecosystem of the street, perception is reality. Their mere presence was a threat.

The OGs decided to act.

It happened after school. Maria, Edwin, and Santos were waiting on the elevated subway platform. The station was ground level, separated from the street by just a chain-link fence and a staircase.

Suddenly, a wave of them came up the stairs - fifteen, maybe twenty guys. The air instantly thickened with testosterone and danger.

Accusations flew. "What set you claim?" "You think you hard?"

Two of them stepped to Santos and Edwin. Two girls cornered Maria. They tried to hold their own, but the math was against them.

Edwin was on the ground, curled in a defensive ball. Santos was being shoved backward, his heels catching on the edge of the platform.

Behind him was the drop to the tracks and the third rail.

This is it, he thought. *I'm going over.*

Then, yelling. Not from them, but from the stairs.

Four cops came charging up. The OGs didn't fight; they scattered. They vaulted off the platform, cleared the fence, and disappeared into the streets of Far Rockaway like smoke.

They were hauled into the school police office. The vibe wasn't "Are you okay?" It was "Talk or walk."

"If you don't press charges," the officer said, "we're charging *you* with public disturbance. Everyone goes down."

The code of silence is strong, but the fear of jail is stronger. They talked.

They identified one of the ringleaders in a photo lineup. They signed the statements. They went home.

The Bridge

A week later, Edwin gathered the crew. "My brother's handling it," he said, his voice dropping an octave. "The OGs are gonna be taken care of. But we need to lay low. Don't take the shuttle. Walk the bridge across the bay."

So they walked. They were soldiers following orders, hiking across the bridge that connected the peninsula to the mainland. The winter wind off the water was biting, cutting through their coats.

Halfway across, they saw a figure walking toward them. All black. Hoodie up. Hands in pockets.

Nothing unusual for winter in Queens. Until he got close.

Click-clack.

The sound of a pistol racking is distinct. It cuts through the wind.

The man pulled a gun. He pointed it first at Edwin, then swung the barrel until it was staring directly between Santos's eyes.

The black hole of the muzzle looked infinite.

"You can take a swim," he said, nodding toward the icy water below, "or you can keep your mouth shut. Your choice."

He didn't wait for an answer. He lowered the gun, walked past them, and disappeared down the bridge.

The Cost of Justice

Weeks later, the subpoena came. The Grand Jury.

Santos had a choice. He could listen to the man on the bridge and keep his mouth shut. Or he could stand up. He could be the person he wanted to be - the guy who didn't let fear dictate his life.

In a glimmer of courage, he went. He put his hand on the Bible. He swore the oath. He told the truth.

He thought he had won. He thought he had beaten the bullies.

Days later, the phone rang. His mother answered. It was the detective.

"Listen," he said, his voice tired. "These guys... they're the real deal. The kids in school are just playing gangster, but their families? This is their life. The rivalry is getting worse. We're calling all the victims."

He paused.

"We think it's best - since Santos lives out of the borough - that you start a 'Safety Transfer.' Get him out of there. Move him to his zoned school in the Bronx."

The transfer happened at the speed of a whirlwind. First came the meeting at the school.

It was his mother, the school counselor, and Santos. Honestly, while they spoke in hushed, serious tones about "threat assessments" and "safety transfers," he just stared into space. He wasn't really sure what was going on, and to be honest, he didn't see what the big deal was.

Isn't this just what the world was like? Growing up in the Bronx, in the areas he did, you heard stories of people getting guns pulled on them all the time. Nine times out of ten, the threats were empty. Yes, there were cold-blooded killers out there, but even they knew that following through on those threats risked a lifetime in prison.

A dumb high school beef wasn't worth risking that freedom. In reality, the jail time would only serve to build his street cred, but the body? That was too much heat. He figured it was a bluff.

He walked out of the office and met up with the crew. When he told them the administration was talking about transferring him, the air left the circle.

Maria's face dropped, and she began to cry immediately.

"It's all good," he told them, putting on the mask of confidence. "The end of the year is still some time away. If things chill out, they probably won't do anything."

But that wasn't the case. The system didn't wait for things to chill.

Within a week, the order came down: *You start the new school next week. You are not going back.*

There was no goodbye hug. No locker clean-out. Just a hard severing.

The first call he made was to Maria. She didn't take it well, but they tried to patch a raft together to survive the distance. They arranged to go out that weekend to the movies, with her mom chaperoning. They clung to that plan, pretending it was just a normal date.

But the drift is a powerful current. It started with biology.

Her mom had Lupus, and a severe flare-up took her out of the picture. Then Maria got appendicitis. Suddenly, the logistics of seeing each other became impossible.

Then came the technology gap. Cell phones existed, but they weren't like today; they were just expensive, glorified house phones. They were at the mercy of the landline. Unless you could afford Call Waiting - which they couldn't - callers would just get a busy signal.

Communicating was left up to chance. It was a lottery of timing, made worse by the warden at home.

His mother didn't like anyone having any type of enjoyment, and long phone calls were a target. "Get off the phone" became the soundtrack of his evenings.

Daily calls turned to weekly. Weekly turned to every couple of weeks. Then, none.

The "break up" was never an actual event. No one ever said the words "it's over." The relationship just drifted into non-existence over time, suffocated by busy signals and missed connections.

He spoke to her one last time over that summer. He sat on the floor of his room, twisting the cord around his finger.

"How are you?"

"Good. You?"

"Good."

It was an awkward set of updating statements. They were two kids who didn't know how to handle the heavy feelings of loss, and they didn't know how to restart the engine that had stalled. It was just easier to ignore the relationship and allow it to fade away.

We hung up, and the line went dead. He didn't know it then, but that silence would be the loudest thing he'd heard in years. The hope that had sparked in the summer was snuffed out. The joy that was growing was smothered.

He learned a bitter lesson that day: Doing the right thing doesn't always save you. Sometimes, it just costs you everything.

He was back in the Bronx. Back to zero. And now, he was angry.

The Planetarium 1995 - The Bronx

He wasn't angry. Anger requires energy. Anger implies that you believe you deserve better and are furious that you aren't getting it.

He didn't feel that. He felt "off." Like a radio tuned slightly between stations - just static and white noise.

The "Safety Transfer" had dropped him into a new high school in the Bronx. If the school in Queens had been a sprawling campus of wings and open air, this place was a factory. It was a rectangular, seven-story brick slab. It felt institutional. It felt like a holding pen for the borough's kids until they were old enough for the workforce or the precinct.

He walked the hallways like a ghost. He didn't try to make friends. He didn't try to stand out. He had learned his lesson in Far Rockaway: *Connection leads to pain. Visibility leads to danger.*

But there was one thing that cut through the static.

On the top floor, there was a dome. A planetarium.

To a kid who had spent his childhood looking up at the sky to escape the reality of the ground, it was a magnet. It was a promise that even here, in this brick box in the Bronx, there was a window to the infinite. It reawakened that spark he had felt when his father taught him about motherboards and meteorology.

He decided to ask for it. It was the only sign of interest he had shown in anything since the transfer.

He sat in the guidance counselor's office. To this day, he couldn't tell you what he looked like. He was a blur of beige and bureaucracy. A man whose job was to manage files, not futures.

"I want to take the astronomy class," Santos said. "The one that uses the dome."

He didn't look up from the folder. He flipped a page, scanning the borderline grades that had transferred over from Queens.

"That's a Junior-level elective," he said, his voice flat. "You're a Freshman. You don't qualify."

"But I know the material," Santos tried to say. "I love science."

"Rules are rules," he said, finally looking at him with dead, tired eyes. "Focus on your core classes. Get your grades up. Maybe in two years."

Two years. In his world, two years was a lifetime. He didn't know where he'd be in two weeks.

He stamped a paper. He sent him back to class.

He didn't know it, but he had just extinguished the last little light Santos was carrying. The system had a wonder right there on the roof, but they kept the door locked.

He went back to class, but he wasn't really there. He sat in the back, the static in his head getting louder.

The Punchline

School ended, and the summer of '95 rolled in like a heatwave.

The Bronx was alive. The streets were dangerous - shootouts were regular, drug dealers owned the corners - but to him, the concrete was safer than the carpet.

Outside, he could dodge. Outside, he could run.

But his mother, gripped by her own anxieties, kept the leash tight. She got an "itch" to keep him inside, locking him in the apartment for days at a time.

He was stuck. Trapped in the air-conditioned cage with the TV on. The only mercy was that his father was working. During the day, the apartment was his. He could breathe. He could exist without the weight of his gaze.

But at 5:00 PM, the key would turn in the lock.

He didn't come home angry. He didn't come home stumbling or shouting. He came home ready to hold court. He would crack open a forty-ounce beer - or two - and the apartment would fill up.

His sister would come over. Neighbors would drop by. The atmosphere was lively. It was loud. There was music and laughter.

And Santos was the prop.

The violence wasn't the dark, hidden assault of the night anymore. It was the open, heavy-handed violence of a "joke."

He would tell a story, holding a cigarette in one hand and a beer in the other. If Santos said something silly, the room would chuckle, and then - *Smack.*

A hard, open hand to the back of the head.

"You're such a clown," he'd say, laughing.

The room would laugh with him.

If he knocked something over or tripped, *Smack.*

"You're such a klutz," he'd roar, grinning.

It was performance art. Santos was the punchline. Because everyone was laughing - because the beer was flowing and the music was playing - it made the violence impossible to name. If he got upset, he was the one ruining the good time. He was the one who "couldn't take a joke."

So he learned to smile while his head throbbed. He learned to laugh while the humiliation burned in his chest.

He sat in the corner of that lively, loud apartment, realizing that the most dangerous place in the world wasn't a dark alley. It was a living room where everyone is laughing at you while you bleed.

1995 - The Bronx, New York

The fight with his father didn't end the war; it just changed the front lines.

At home, the dynamic had shifted into a cold, uneasy detente. But outside the apartment, Santos was drifting.

He was fifteen years old, now attending Harrison High - a sprawling, overcrowded warehouse of a school - but "attending" was a generous word. He was a ghost in the hallways. He didn't have a clique. He didn't have a team.

He barely had a GPA.

He spent more time cutting class than sitting in it. The education system had long ago labeled him as "one of those kids" - the kind you push through the system until they either drop out or age out.

The future being laid out for him was grimly predictable.

His mother, trapping him in the kitchen or the living room, would lay out her vision for his adulthood. It wasn't a vision of college or a career.

"We need to get things moving," she would say, her voice tight with the anxiety of poverty. "We need to get you signed up for the work programs so you can get assistance when you get older."

It was a legacy of dependence. She was handing him the baton in a relay race to the welfare office.

I don't want this, Santos thought. The thought was quiet, but it was stubborn. *I don't want to be you.*

But he didn't know how to be anyone else.

The intervention didn't come from a social worker or a guidance counselor. It came from his cousin. She was the daughter of the uncle who had once sent him packing - the same uncle who had looked at the chaos of Santos's mother and closed the door to protect his own family.

It was a strange irony that the salvation came from the same house that had delivered the rejection.

She looked at Santos's grades, his truancy, and the glazed look in his eyes, and she refused to let him drown.

"There's a school," she told him. "An alternative high school. I think you should apply."

"Alternative" usually meant "reform." It was usually where the bad kids went before prison. But she insisted. This place was different.

The commute didn't take him out of the Bronx. He still got on the public bus, watching the familiar grit of the city roll by through scratched plexiglass windows. The streets were the same. The noise was the same. But when he stepped off the bus and walked into the building, the atmosphere changed.

It wasn't chaos. It wasn't a holding cell. It was an institution of intent.

The shock came in homeroom.

The teacher was a man who didn't fit the zip code. He was the math teacher, Santos's worst subject, and by all appearances, he belonged in a corporate boardroom or a manicured suburb. He lived in New Jersey, commuting hours every day to cross the bridge into the Bronx.

He didn't *have* to be here. He had money. He had status. In Santos's experience, people with money avoided the Bronx. This man drove straight into it.

The orientation wasn't a lecture on rules. It wasn't a threat about attendance policies or metal detectors. The teacher set up the room for interviews. He sat with every single student, one by one.

When it was Santos's turn, he didn't open a file folder. He didn't look at the transcripts filled with Fs and absences. He didn't ask about the disciplinary record.

He looked Santos in the eye.

"What are your goals?" he asked.

Santos blinked. No one had ever asked him that. They had asked *where were you?* or *why didn't you do the homework?* or *did you fill out the forms?*

"I don't know," Santos said.

"What are the obstacles?" the teacher asked. "What is stopping you from succeeding?"

For the first time, an adult wasn't looking at what Santos had done wrong. He was looking at what Santos could do right. He was investing.

It wasn't just him. The school was filled with them - teachers who cared, some of whom were alumni who had sat in these same desks and made it out. They returned not to brag, but to pull others up.

The philosophy of the school was radical in its simplicity: *Your past is not your future.*

In that classroom, sitting across from the man from New Jersey, the "Charity Kid" began to die. The shame of the food stamps and the welfare applications faded.

For the first time, Santos wasn't waiting for a handout. He was being offered a blueprint.

And he decided to build.

The Buyback 1997-1999

At seventeen, the script finally flipped.

He had been transferred to an alternative school, and for the first time, the system seemed to work *with* him rather than against him.

The fog lifted. His grades skyrocketed - actual A's and B's. He wasn't the invisible kid in the back anymore; he was on the baseball team. He was in student government. Things started to feel like they were supposed to.

But the real education wasn't happening in the classroom. It was happening in his bank account.

He had learned a hard lesson the previous summer, at sixteen.

His mother had enrolled him in a government assistance program for low-income youth. His assignment was cleaning Orchard Beach. It was brutal, humbling work - raking trash and debris out of the scorching sand.

He did it because he wanted the money. But when the check came, he never saw a dime.

His mother took it.

"You owe me," she would say, snapping the check out of his hand. "I feed you. I buy you clothes. This is *my* money."

It was her go-to line whenever she needed to counter him. He was "good for nothing." Every request was framed as, "Can you do me a *special favor*?" followed by "Get off your ass and stop being lazy."

She would say this while she sat on the sofa for eight hours straight, glued to the TV, watching her "stories." The hypocrisy burned hotter than the sun at Orchard Beach.

He was the one sweating in the sand, but he was the "lazy" one.

He vowed that wouldn't happen again.

The Marathon

At seventeen, he found his own way. He applied for a warehouse job with the Marathon Club in the South Bronx. They handled all the merchandise for the marathon runners.

This wasn't government assistance. This was a job.

Every day that summer, he went down to the South Bronx. He clocked in. He moved heavy boxes in the humid heat. It was hard labor, but it was honest.

And most importantly, the check came in *his* name.

When summer ended, his assignment was over, but he had worked hard enough that they kept his info. When the Marathon Expo weekend approached, they called him back.

"Can you join the team for the weekend?" they asked.

"I'm there," he said.

It was a grueling three-day sprint - Friday night, all day Saturday, and most of Sunday. We worked the tables, managing the chaos of thousands of runners picking up their gear. We clocked close to thirty hours in three days.

He was exhausted, but when that check hit his hand, the fatigue vanished.

There was no "this is my money" from his mother this time. She couldn't touch it. He had earned it in a world she didn't control.

The Investment

He didn't just save the money. He used it to change the power dynamic in the house.

He walked into an electronics store and bought a 32-inch TV. In the late 90s, that was a heavy, massive box - a monolith of success. He carried it home. He set it up. It was undeniable proof that he wasn't "good for nothing."

But the real power move wasn't the TV. It was the food.

He started buying groceries for the house. He started taking them out to dinner.

"My treat," he would say, putting the cash on the table.

It felt good. It felt like armor. She couldn't call him lazy when he was feeding her. She couldn't say he owed her when he was the one paying the bill.

He had tasted a little bit of freedom, and he knew that this was the way.

The Pivot

He graduated at eighteen. In January of 1999, he followed the "correct" path and enrolled in college.

But the taste of independence was too strong. During the summer of '99, he started working part-time at a currency exchange.

He was good at it. He understood numbers. He understood value.

By mid-fall of 1999, he looked at the slow grind of college, and then he looked at the paycheck from the currency exchange.

He made a calculation.

He dropped out. He went full-time.

The "Charity Kid" who waited for handouts was dead. The "Soldier" who took orders was still forming. But in that moment, The Investor was born. He was betting on himself.

CHAPTER 7
THE GREY GRIND

1999–2001 Manhattan, New York

The blueprint from the alternative school had a flaw: it assumed the rest of the world operated like the school.

It didn't.

Santos graduated with the "Pending Grade" resolved and a diploma in his hand, buoyed by the belief that he had finally cracked the code. He enrolled in college, expecting the same dynamic he had just left - the "invested authority," the teachers who looked you in the eye and asked about your obstacles.

Instead, he walked into a lecture hall of three hundred ghosts. The professors didn't know his name. They didn't care about his backstory. They handed out the syllabus like indictments: *Here is the work. Do it or don't.*

The scaffolding of support - the very thing that had allowed Santos to climb out of the academic hole - vanished overnight.

He was back in the "Cold Accountability" system, and without the external pressure to succeed, the internal drive sputtered. He stopped going. The failure wasn't a crash; it was a drift. He simply faded out of the roster, another statistic in a city full of them.

But the "Charity Kid" was dead. He couldn't go back to dependency. He needed money. He needed a job.

He found himself in the belly of the beast: Wall Street.

He lived with his mother for a short time when he first started at the currency exchange, but as soon as he transitioned to full-time work, he made his move. He rented a furnished apartment in the West Bronx - a place where he didn't have to worry about the immediate burden of buying furniture.

It was a crucial vacuum of space for him, a time to finally figure himself out without the constant, atmospheric chaos that had defined every home he'd ever known.

His life expanded into the digital world. This was the era of AOL, and he spent hours building a circle of "online friends" and navigating the early world of dating. In the environment he came from, serious relationships were often mocked as being "locked down" or "whipped," so he kept everything casual.

He'd go on dates and talk on the phone, but he never committed to anyone specific.

On the weekends, if the weather was clear, he'd take long walks from the heart of the West Bronx up to the bustling shopping hubs. He'd stop in to visit his mother, hang out with friends from the old neighborhood, and then retreat back to the sanctuary of his own walls.

The address was a weapon in itself. Working on Wall Street meant you had arrived. It meant you were part of the engine that turned the world.

Santos landed a job at a major international currency firm, handling foreign exchange for high-net-worth clients and corporate accounts. The office was reminiscent of a large ticket window of a stadium, with a large executive office in the back and a massive safe anchored in the corner. The contrast was notable: you had entry-level customer service in the front and middle management visible right behind the glass.

The commute to that office was a long, grinding odyssey. Because he needed to be at the window early, he was usually on the train before the express lines started running. It was a slow, stop-and-go crawl through the entire length of the city.

On those long local rides, he began to construct a new identity.

He still carried the heavy Bronx accent and a vocabulary that hadn't yet caught up to his ambition, but he was a sponge. Once he stepped off the train and walked into that office, he put on his newly acquired personality.

He started to notice that the world around him wasn't the world of slang or the exaggerated, loud outbursts typical of the block back home. His voice was naturally projected, and he'd catch the sideways looks from the pinstriped "Ghosts" who judged him as an outsider infiltrating their world.

He didn't let it stop him. He learned. Every morning, he'd pick up the newspaper and spend the day reading the news whenever there was a lull at the window. He tuned his radio to the popular morning talk shows. They were a bright spot in the grind - men who were funny and seemingly carefree.

He remembered listening to them and thinking, *I don't know what world they live in that they can be so happy, but I want to be a part of it.*

It wasn't the movies - there were no power suits, no screaming trading floors, no illicit substances in the bathrooms - but it wasn't the DMV, either. There was a pulse to it. The job offered tiny, addictive tastes of adrenaline.

It was the rush of holding a brick of yen worth fifty thousand dollars. It was the friction of the thumb counting through a stack of fresh pounds. It was the ticker tape scrolling across the bottom of the screen, a red and green river that dictated the fortunes of nations.

The day's work was often mundane, but it required total vigilance.

You came in and counted yourself into your till, ensuring you had the main currencies in "stock" for the day. You booted up the currency exchange software and ensured the starting rates - this was where a day could go from mundane to catastrophic.

Many currencies could cause a massive loss if you misplaced the decimal by one spot or entered a 1 versus a 2. The anchor point rate was sent daily to each office via spreadsheet, and once that rate was entered, the computer adjusted for market changes throughout the day. Only during massive shifts in the wholesale rate did you go back in and change the rate manually.

If you entered the wrong rate to start with and weren't experienced enough to realize the spread of each currency, the whole day would bleed profit. While an error could occasionally favor the company, typical customers pointed out the discrepancy immediately.

However, if the rate favored the customer, they wouldn't say anything. Instead, they would talk you up to distract you even more, sometimes even sending friends and family to hit the same window while the mistake was live.

When he first started, this happened to him on a small scale; he never took too much of a loss, but the worry of it stayed in the back of his head, a constant mental audit he carried every time he opened the till.

When the markets moved, the phone lines lit up. You had to be fast. You had to be precise.

For a few minutes at a time, during a market spike, Santos felt like a pilot in a cockpit, flipping switches, moving capital, riding the wave.

But the wave always crashed. The rush would fade, leaving behind the silence of the cage.

His world shrank down to a two-man ecosystem. His partner in the branch was Russo - a guy in his late thirties who treated the financial sector with the casual indifference of a mechanic fixing a carburetor. Russo was a creature of simple, sturdy habits. He worshipped at the altar of AC/DC, and his culinary horizon began and ended with a medium-rare ribeye.

Russo was his stepping stone into what he would call middle-class America. He wasn't middle class himself, and he wasn't polished or proper in the slightest, but he also wasn't uneducated. He didn't speak in slang or curse excessively like everyone back in the Bronx.

Russo lived with his mother; he always said it was because of her health, which Santos was sure was true, but he reaped the benefits of the arrangement. She cooked and cleaned, and he provided the money - a symbiotic relationship they had both settled into.

Russo didn't have a wife or kids and seemed entirely uninterested in seeking them out. He didn't do himself any favors in the dating department; he usually reeked of cigarette smoke and looked like he'd rolled out of bed and into his work clothes. But if any woman had taken the time to look past the "fixer-upper" exterior, they would have found a man who would have hand-sewn a red carpet for them.

He was the type of guy who would literally give you the shirt off his back.

They worked well together. It was an easy, masculine camaraderie. They split the window duties, shared the admin work, and passed the lull times debating whether *Back in Black* or *Highway to Hell* was the superior album.

It was like hanging out with one of the guys, except you were handling millions of dollars.

And Santos was good at it. Better than he expected. His brain, which had rejected the abstract theories of college, latched onto the tactical reality of the market. He began to see the matrix behind the numbers.

He knew the ghetto, full of drugs and shootouts. The welfare life of Medicaid and food stamps wasn't for him. He wanted more.

He knew that people back in the neighborhood would call him a "coconut" - brown on the outside, white on the inside - even if his skin was lighter than most. He didn't care about being a "sellout." He always wondered how people who had absolutely nothing could talk about "selling" anything.

It was around this time that reality changed for him.

He started realizing that the false pride of the streets - that "Puerto Rican Pride" or "New York Pride" - was actually an anchor designed to hold people down. As long as you thought trying to better yourself was a betrayal of your roots, you would never escape the situation you were in. He loved the island, but he realized that a pride that causes you to denounce anything different is just a handicap.

Gaining this insight pushed him to broaden his knowledge. The change wasn't overnight, but slowly, he was learning to be more business casual and less "cheese line."

He began to see that while the firm was massive, the people running the accounts were often asleep at the wheel. Russo was the exception. He could rattle off currency rates after looking at them just once in the morning. He was so good at his job that he was one of only three people in the entire company with the authority to change rates to land a larger deal.

Eventually, after proving his own competence in calculating margins - giving a client just enough of a break to land the deal while ensuring a substantial spread for profit - Santos became one of those three as well.

Russo's "don't give a fuck" attitude had a lasting impact on him. He saw that he knew his stuff and he knew his value; he could do the work of two or three people at his peak. That expertise was his armor.

There was one day Santos showed up to work without a tie.

Ties were a non-negotiable mandate from the District Manager (DM), a man who lived to dock pay for minor infractions. If he saw you on camera or caught you during a surprise visit without one, he'd send you home to get it, dock your day's pay, and make you come back even if there was only one minute left on the clock.

We got word that the DM was on his way, and Santos started to panic. Commuting was an anxiety-driven nightmare for him, and he couldn't afford a lost day.

Without a word, Russo reached up, took off his own clip-on tie, and told him to wear it. Santos tried to refuse, but he insisted.

A few minutes later, the DM waltzed in through the back entrance. The first thing he said was, "Russo, where is your tie?"

"Forgot it, boss," Russo said, leaning back with total indifference.

The DM rolled his eyes. "Well, I would send you home, but I know you would just tell me 'fuck you' and go have a smoke. So do not forget your tie next time or else I will dock you for your smoke breaks."

"No worries, boss," Russo replied. He grabbed his pack, walked out, and lit one up.

Russo had worked at the company longer than anyone, including the DM. He could have been a Regional Manager, but he was happy where he was. That lesson stayed with Santos: know your value so well that the rules intended for those who need control don't apply to you.

It's a philosophy he carries today. Even now, navigating cognitive issues that have dropped his work accuracy from 99.8% to 98.9%, he maintains his own processes. He noticed the issue and created his own crutch to ensure he maintains his standard.

He learned that self-reliance from Russo in the Cage.

The "Spice" came from the hunt. The firm relied on massive contracts with the hospitality giants - hotels that needed millions in currency liquidity for their international clientele.

One afternoon, a crisis alert flashed. The Cosmopolitan Hotel - one of their whales - was threatening to walk. A competitor was undercutting their rates.

Santos didn't just pass the memo. He opened the hood. He dug into the transaction logs and found the anomaly. The account manager assigned to The Cosmopolitan had been coasting. He was using a "set-and-forget" strategy, updating the exchange rates once a week instead of riding the daily fluctuations.

The market had dipped, but The Cosmopolitan was still paying last week's premium. They were bleeding cash because of a lazy algorithm.

Santos saw the opening. He didn't ask for permission. He picked up the phone and bypassed the account manager. He called the hotel's Controller directly.

"I see the bleed," Santos told him. "Your rates are stale. I'm fixing it now."

He manually overrode the system. He keyed in the live market rate - a razor-thin margin that undercut the competitor but kept the profit volume high. He didn't just stop the bleeding; he reversed the flow.

"Check your feed," Santos said.

There was a silence on the line. Then, a grunt of approval. "That's better. That's much better."

Santos didn't just save the account; he stole it. He became the go-to guy for the fix.

Later, he used that same aggressive precision to land the Sterling Trust account, walking into a meeting he had no business being in and closing the deal with the confidence of a veteran.

Because of this competence, he was eventually put on a schedule that rotated him between four different offices - Midtown, Wall Street, Columbus Circle, and a branch in Connecticut - depending on where they needed someone with the skill to handle high-traffic issues or complex accounts.

For a moment, the adrenaline was real. He had hunted. He had killed. He had brought home the prize.

He walked out onto Wall Street, the wind whipping through the canyons of steel and glass, feeling the power of the city in his chest. He was twenty-one. He was a player.

But by the summer of 2001, the victories began to taste like ash. The adrenaline of the trade was fleeting. Saving a hotel money wasn't the same as saving a life. Moving numbers on a screen wasn't the same as moving mountains.

The "Grey Grind" wasn't grey because it was boring; it was grey because it was hollow.

He would walk out at lunch, tilting his head back to see the Twin Towers scraping the sky, shining like tuning forks for the universe. The city was invincible. He was successful. He should have been happy. But the silence inside him was growing louder.

The "Warrior" he had discovered when he punched his father was pacing inside a cage made of pinstripes and spreadsheets. He was a weapon sitting on a shelf, gathering dust.

The mundane nature of the grind was retroactively shattered in the weeks following the September 11th attacks.

Management returned to the Midtown office - where he had been working on and off during the Labor Day rush - and began pulling archives for the FBI. It was discovered that one of the lead hijackers had cashed travelers' checks at their window.

He had been working that day, though he wasn't the one who processed that specific transaction. He eventually had to provide testimony to the FBI about the day's events. It yielded nothing; he didn't remember anything unusual because his day had been as mundane as every other.

For a long time, he kept a photocopy of those travelers' checks - a physical reminder of how close the shadow had passed - but that was thrown away years later when his ex-fiance purged his military records.

He felt like he was waiting for a bell to ring. He didn't know that the bell was already swinging. He didn't know that the "Grey Grind" was about to end in a cloud of dust that would choke the entire world.

He didn't know that he only had a few weeks left of being a civilian.

CHAPTER 8
THE TWILIGHT ZONE

September 11, 2001 - The Bronx, New York

Survival often comes down to the smallest, most irritating variables. In Iraq, it would be a seating chart. In New York, it was a set of keys.

On the morning of the eleventh, Santos wasn't supposed to be in the Bronx. He was scheduled to be at the currency branch near the Battery, standing in the cage with Russo, trading yen for dollars. But the night before, a coworker from the Connecticut office - who happened to be a family friend - had gone home with the wrong set of keys.

It was a mundane, clerical screw-up. The kind that usually resulted in a groan and an eye-roll. The call from the manager came early, explaining that time was of the essence due to the train schedules. Santos grabbed a local cab from his apartment and headed to the Metro North station. His mother lived only a few blocks from the tracks, and he intended to head to her place after the exchange; his bedroom there was still set up for the nights he stayed over to help out.

The exchange at the station was pleasant. Santos handed over the master keys so the Connecticut branch could open. He waited with the coworker for the train, which arrived in minutes. Because the commute would make him three hours late for the city, his manager made the call:

"Just take the day off, Santos. We'll cover the window."

It was a gift. A Tuesday off in September. Normally, September in New York is the mouth of fall - gloomy clouds and consistent rain. But this morning was absolutely beautiful. It was the kind of weather that made people wake up a little happier.

The parks were filling with kids. Even the neighborhood thugs were out playing handball against the brick walls instead of looking for trouble. It was a day that seemed to have nothing but promise.

Santos walked to his mother's apartment, ignorant that the first plane had already hit. He thought about breakfast, thinking about sleeping in, thinking about the Sterling Trust deal he had just closed.

He didn't know that with every step he took up the stairs to his mother's door, a firefighter in lower Manhattan was taking a step up the stairs of the World Trade Center. They were both moving toward a world where America was no longer invincible.

He turned on the TV.

The image didn't make sense. The North Tower - the building he looked up at every day during lunch - had a black gash in its side. Smoke was pouring out, staining the perfect blue sky.

"We have reports of a plane..." the news anchor said, their voice steady but confused.

A small plane, Santos thought. *Some idiot in a Cessna got lost.* It was the only logical explanation. The Towers were massive; you couldn't miss them. It had to be an accident.

He stood there, remote in hand, checking the time. It was 9:02 AM. Russo would be at the window. Elena, the fill-in for the day, would be counting out the drawers. They were right there.

Then, he saw it.

From the right side of the screen, a grey shape appeared. It wasn't a Cessna. It was a Boeing 767. It banked hard, the sun glinting off the fuselage - a flash of silver before the black.

It slammed into the South Tower.

The explosion wasn't just on the screen; it felt like it happened in the room. The fireball erupted, blowing debris out the other side of the building. The remote dropped from Santos's hand.

The thought formed instantly, bypassing denial and landing straight on the truth.

"Oh my god," he whispered to the empty room. "We are at war."

Then the house shook. It wasn't an earthquake. It was a roar - a sound so loud it vibrated the fillings in his teeth.

BOOM. BOOM.

Santos ran to the window. Two F-15 fighter jets tore through the sky directly over his roof, afterburners glowing, banking hard toward Manhattan.

They were flying combat patrol over the Bronx.

That was the moment the "Twilight Zone" began.

He grabbed the phone. He dialed the branch number. *Beep-beep-beep.* "All circuits are busy." He dialed Russo's cell. *Beep-beep-beep.* "All circuits are busy." He dialed his cousin, who worked in Midtown. *Beep-beep-beep.*

The silence of the phone was more terrifying than the noise on the TV. He ran outside.

The Bronx was a borough defined by noise - sirens, car horns, shouting, the constant hum of millions of people living on top of each other. But when he stepped onto the sidewalk, the world was dead.

It was a frightening, heavy silence. The flight path to LaGuardia, usually a highway of commercial jets, was empty. The sky was naked. The streets were deserted. No one was walking dogs. No one was arguing over parking spots.

The only sound was the distant, rhythmic roar of the fighters circling the city like sharks.

Everything for the next few days was a blur. The offices were shut down, and Santos stayed at his mother's house. The buses weren't running, and he couldn't peel himself away from the television long enough to walk back to his own apartment. Many people in the neighborhood were the same; no one wanted to be alone, even if it meant returning to a chaotic environment.

The silence of those nights was eerie. It was like camping in the middle of the city; you could hear bugs and birds chirping because the city sounds had evaporated. No pops from guns, no sirens chasing robbery suspects. Even the neighbors who argued every night were silent.

Santos sat on the porch, smelling the air. He wondered if the noxious scent was the smoke from the site drifting north, or if his mind was just playing tricks on him.

He remained obsessed with the screen. In the middle of the night, he would unmute the TV just to see if the world had changed again. He stayed in that pause until the day the news cycle finally broke for a commercial.

It felt like the world was coming unpaused. Limited bus routes restarted. Subways began a slow crawl. Bridges opened, allowing people to retrieve vehicles they had abandoned in the panic.

He climbed to the roof of his building, looking south. There it was.

A column of black smoke, thick and oily, rising from the tip of the island. It looked like a chimney stack for hell. It wasn't just smoke; it was the city burning.

The stories trickled in over the next few days, pieced together as the phone lines opened up.

Russo and Elena had exited the subway station at Rector Street just as the first plane hit. They were standing at the foot of the giants. Elena, seeing the fire, had frozen. She stared up, mesmerized by the debris raining down.

"Look at the pieces," she had told Russo later, her voice hollow. "The building is falling apart."

Russo, older and sharper, had grabbed her arm and dragged her away. He knew what she didn't want to see.

Those weren't pieces of the building. They were people. They were jumping to escape the heat, falling a thousand feet to the pavement where Santos usually bought his lunch.

His cousin told a different story. She had been in Midtown, miles away, but the panic wave hit them all the same. She described walking out of her building into a blizzard of paper and ash. She described the "Grey People" - men in thousand-dollar suits covered in dust, walking north like zombies, eyes blank, carrying briefcases they no longer needed.

On the Monday following the attacks, management organized a retrieval operation.

Santos and another handler were tasked with going down to the Wall Street branch to empty the safe. It felt poorly planned to Santos - two young men on the subway carrying laptop bags filled with nearly half a million dollars in global currency, gold coins, and silver bars.

When they exited the subway at the final stop, the smell hit them.

It was a noxious, metallic taste that sat in the back of the throat and made the sinuses burn. Santos's eyes were bloodshot within minutes. A heavy fog entered his brain, similar to the lightheadedness of high altitude.

Inside the branch, the office was buried under a quarter-inch of grey dust. It looked like ruins that had been left for centuries, even though humans had been there less than a week prior.

They worked quickly, grabbing the currency and the backup digital drives. They flipped the breakers to the off position to prevent power surges from starting a fire in the ruins.

As they headed back toward the checkpoint, Santos took a mental picture of the scene.

The National Guard had become a fixture near the site. Humvees sat on the corners. The soldiers looked like they were in an apocalyptic movie - their uniforms showed wear, their boots had lost their gloss. Their rifles hung from their necks, hands resting lightly on the grips.

It was their eyes that stopped him. They were eighteen and nineteen-year-old kids with seventy-year-old eyes. They had developed the thousand-yard stare in a single week.

Santos wondered if at the end of that stare was Afghanistan or Iraq. They had a focus in their non-focus. They had found a target; they only needed the fog of war to clear so they could engage.

Santos absorbed every story, every sight. With every detail, a cold weight settled in his chest.

I should have been there.

It wasn't a wish for death; it was a debt. He had been spared by a set of keys. He was safe in the Bronx while Russo was dragging Elena through the fallout. He was watching fighters patrol his neighborhood, realizing for the first time that the "New York Rican" flag on his hoodie wasn't enough.

He had spent his life distrusting the government, seeing "The System" as the enemy. But as he watched the smoke rise, that identity fractured. Those weren't government buildings falling. That was his city. That was his skyline.

He realized that morning was the last time he would ever be a "normal" person.

The hope of overcoming his family trauma and the abuse he'd endured at the hands of his parents felt like a secondary concern now. That was trauma he believed he could have faced and overcome in time. But the new trauma - the realization that his world was falling - shattered that possibility.

He wasn't going to stand by. He allowed the Santos of that morning to fall so a new version could rise.

He sat in the silence of his apartment, the "Grey Grind" of currency exchange feeling suddenly, pathetically small. He couldn't go back to the cage. He couldn't sit behind a window selling yen while his city was a graveyard.

The "Charity Kid" had spent his life surviving. The "Warrior" was about to volunteer.

He looked at the phone. He didn't call a recruiter that day - the lines were still spotty, the world still burning - but the contract was already signed in his head.

He wasn't going back to Elite Currency. He was going to war.

It was May of 2002. Santos had already signed the contract.

His birthday was coming up, so he arranged a lunch at a steakhouse off Fordham Road. He invited everyone - his mother, his father, his aunt, his cousin, and her husband. It started well. We were laughing, eating, drinking. The bill was going to be over three hundred dollars, but he didn't care.

It was a small price to pay for the grenade he was about to toss onto the table.

The food arrived, steaming and smelling of garlic and charred beef. He tapped his glass.

"Before we start eating, I have something I need to tell everyone," he said. The table went quiet. "A few months ago, I made a big decision. I didn't tell anyone because I didn't want anyone to discourage me or try to change my mind. I joined the Army National Guard."

The silence was absolute. It was a group of people who usually lacked the ability to stop talking, yet they learned how in a single heartbeat.

The first to speak, predictably, was his mother. "You're the only child," she said, her voice carrying that familiar, suffocating air of authority. "They can't let you sign up."

It wasn't a question; it was a statement of her own reality, facts be damned.

"Well, Ma, I signed up already. I don't go to Basic until March, but the contract is signed."

"What did you sign up to do?" someone asked.

"Infantry," Santos said, the pride swelling in his chest.

"What is that?"

"Combat. Grunt."

He saw the shift in their eyes - the rising panic, the mobilizing of the "family mob" led by his aunt. He knew if he didn't manage this, they would be driving to the recruiter's office within the hour to demand the contract be ripped up.

So, he did what he had learned to do to survive in that house. He lied.

"But it's the National Guard," he added quickly, waving a hand dismissively. "We only get called as a last resort. The main job for us is storms, floods, things like that. We hardly ever go to war."

"Since you haven't gone to Basic yet," his aunt said, the gears of manipulation already turning, "that means you can have them cancel the contract, right?"

They didn't see a 22-year-old man with his own apartment. They saw a possession that was slipping out of their control. But for the first time, their grip didn't hold.

He paid the bill, he smiled, and he went home.

A year later, at 3:00 AM on a humid July morning in 2003, his recruiter pulled up to the curb.

Santos put his bag on his shoulder, walked out of his mother's house, and got into the car. As we pulled away, the distance between the car and that house grew, putting space between the end of the manipulation and a future that - for the first time - was in his own hands.

CHAPTER 9
THE ONE-LUNG SERGEANT

March–July 2003 Fort Benning, Georgia

War started on television. Santos missed it because he was in a coma.

He had arrived at Fort Benning in March, just as the invasion of Iraq was kicking off. The world was watching "Shock and Awe," viewing the green-tinted night vision footage of Baghdad burning.

But his war was internal.

It started in Week 2. The "Benning Cough" was a rite of passage, a hacking, wet bark that echoed through the barracks at night. But for him, the cough didn't stop at the throat; it settled deep in his chest, heavy and wet like concrete setting in his lungs.

It was first thing in the morning and they were on the PT field. Everyone had a cough to some degree at this point, but that morning he woke up and felt like there was a cement block on his chest.

Suck it up, he remembered thinking. *This wasn't going to be another item in my life that I showed regret.*

He would either push through or he would die. There was no in-between.

The two-mile run was the slowest since his first day at reception. The Drill Sergeant noticed immediately.

"Santos, get the lead out your ass and move!"

"Yes, Drill Sergeant!"

His brain told his legs to pump harder, but they felt like Play-Doh left out overnight. Dinner from the night before was tickling the back of his throat.

"Santos! WHAT IS YOUR MALFUNCTION? ARE YOU MISSING SUCKLING ON YOUR MOMMAS TIT FOR BREAKFAST?"

"NO DRILL SERGEANT!" he tried to say, but it came out as a moaning grunt.

The field was spinning, but he saw the finish line.

"Santos, FOR FUCKS SAKE! BIN LADEN IS GROWING IMPATIENT. YOU THINK YOU CAN GET YOUR STUBBY ASS MOVING SO WE CAN SHOW HIM SOME GOOD OLD AMERICAN HOSPITALITY?"

He barely breathed as he passed the finish line. He ignored the fact that he didn't finish the response.

"FALL IN YOU SORRY SACKS OF SHIT," came from another instructor. "FRONT LEANING REST POSITION... MOVE!"

One, two, three... ONE! One, two, three... TWO!

The cadence continued. He did not. He remembered the grass eating his face.

He heard the Drill Sergeant bark, "What the fuck, Santos?" and then the shout that changed everything: "MEDIC!"

The medics sent him to the infirmary on base. It was supposed to be a "recover and return" situation - three days of rest and meds.

It wasn't rest. It was a descent. He remembered laying on his back, a medic rubbing his sternum. "Take this."

He opened his mouth; the sip of water felt like water hitting baked dry sand. Sternum. Water. Sand.

Rinse and repeat.

By the end of day two in the infirmary, the medics couldn't wake him to administer the pills. He was a dead weight in the cot, burning up from the inside. They hooked him to an IV drip, pumping antibiotics directly into the vein, hoping to flush the infection.

It didn't work.

On the morning of Day 4, they made the call to get him out.

He was loaded into an ambulance, a siren wailing through the training grounds where other recruits were learning to march.

He woke up in the hospital later that day. The room was white. The air was sterile and cold - a sharp contrast to the humid sweat-box of the infirmary. He blinked, trying to scrape the film from his eyes. There were tubes in his arm. A machine beeped a steady, reassuring rhythm next to his head.

A doctor stood at the foot of the bed, reading a chart. He looked up, not with a smile, but with a look of professional relief.

"Welcome back," the doctor said. "Well, son, that was a bit of a scare you gave us. You cut it close. Full infiltration. If they had waited another few hours to bring you in... well, we wouldn't be having this conversation."

He tried to speak, but his throat was sandpaper. He rasped something unintelligible.

Survival had come down to a clock ticking in someone else's hand.

He spent the next two days in a fog, drifting in and out of consciousness. By Day 6, the haze cleared enough for him to understand the cost.

He looked at himself in the bathroom mirror. The "Warrior" he had started to build was gone. He had arrived at Benning a solid 175 pounds of muscle and potential. The reflection staring back was a ghost - hollow-cheeked, ribs showing, weighing in at barely 145. The pneumonia had eaten thirty pounds of mass in less than a week.

On Day 8, the phone in his room rang. He picked it up.

"Well shit, there you are Santos." It was his Drill Sergeant.

He didn't have his "field" voice, but he was still stern. "We were about to mark you AWOL."

"Drill Sergeant?" he questioned, his voice still rough.

"Well, you didn't report that you were transferred to the hospital. When we went to check on you in the infirmary, no one knew where you were."

"Uh, well, I didn't know I was in the hospital either until a few days ago, Drill Sergeant."

"What's that?"

"Well, I guess I took a nap for a few days. I figured the hospital would call, all things considered."

He knew he'd pay for that mouth later, but the Sergeant didn't bite. "Understood. Who's your doctor?"

He read the first name he saw on the wall. "Alright, when they discharge you, report directly to CQ."

It was another five days of recovery before his oxygen levels returned to normal and he could hold down solid food.

On Day 13, they discharged him. He called a cab and pulled into CQ to sign back in. He was directed to the barracks.

Drill was waiting; he had stayed back while the associate Drills took the platoon on a field exercise.

"Santos!" he called as soon as he opened the door. Santos double-timed it to his office.

"Pvt. Santos report - "

"Stow it, Santos. Enter and relax."

He thought it was a trap. He stood at Parade Rest. He was alive, but he was depleted. And the Army doesn't wait for ghosts.

"We have a decision to make, Santos. Usually we just recycle people that have missed this much time, but it is also early enough that you might be able to make it all up. Here's the deal: I am willing to keep you here, but you will have to train with the next class when they do what you missed. So far the only major thing you missed was the CS chamber, but you are on profile for at least another week and you will miss two major ruck marches and a PT Test. You also have some classes that you will need to make up. This is a lot, and you will not get any extra time or miss any of your current training. If you fall out, it will be back to Day One with a new company. Your choice."

The Senior Drill Sergeant was a legend - a man who had taken a bullet through the lung in Grenada and kept fighting. He breathed with a subtle wheeze, a constant reminder that the human body could endure more than it should.

Santos looked at the man with one lung. If he could command a company with half a respiratory system, Santos could finish with two healing ones.

"I'm staying, Drill Sergeant."

"Alright, get in your bunk. You have two days of bed rest and four days of low activity. After that, the medics will see you and we will get you on schedule."

"Yes, Drill Sergeant." The exchange had taken everything out of him.

He watched him leave for the field, donning his cover. He closed his eyes for thirty minutes, then got up and cleaned the latrines.

The next ten weeks were a blur of agony. While the platoon slept, he studied. While they rested, he cleaned barracks, refusing to sit even when the medical profile allowed it.

He rebuilt his body calorie by calorie, pushup by pushup. But the weight didn't come back fast enough. By graduation week, the training had stripped him even further down to a wire-thin 135 pounds.

The bond with Sgt. Graves deepened during a three-day field exercise late in the cycle. That evening it started raining.

One of the instructors yelled, "It's going to rain all night! Enjoy the shower, boys!"

Everyone, including Sgt. Graves, pulled out bars of soap and stripped down.

It was the first time we saw him out of uniform.

Across his chest was a nearly foot-long scar from the sternum, under the chest, and around the ribs. He realized then that comparing his infection to his gunshot wound was a gross misunderstanding of the fight he had endured.

But Graves saw the fight in each of us. He didn't see numbers; he saw the recruits who refused to give up.

The final test was the Ruck March. Week 13. Twenty-five miles. Full battle rattle. A rucksack that weighed nearly half of his current body weight.

By mile three, the platoon hit an obstacle - a concrete wall. We were moving in squad sizes, boosting each other over.

He was hoisted up by the biggest guy in the squad, but the lift was too aggressive. He was yanked over the top.

CRACK.

His shin slammed into the sharp concrete corner of the wall. The pain was a blinding white flash. He hit the ground on the other side, gasping, clutching his leg.

"Move out!" the command came down the line. He stood up. The leg held. It screamed, but it held.

The march became a hallucination. By mile twenty, his body began to disintegrate. The rain from the previous week had turned the trails to mud, and the moisture had seeped into his boots. The skin on the soles of his feet began to slough off, sliding around inside his socks like wet paper.

His toes, numb from the impact, were broken. He wouldn't know until he took his boots off later, but the bones had fractured under the weight.

Mile twenty-two. The wall.

The pain in his shin was a constant, shrieking siren. His lungs, scarred from the pneumonia, burned for oxygen.

He began to drift. He watched the reflective "cat-eyes" on the helmet of the soldier in front of him blur and sway.

He fell back. Ten yards. Twenty yards. He was drifting toward the "Fallout Truck."

The shame was heavier than the ruck. *I can't do it. I'm broken.*

Then, a hand grabbed his ruck frame. It was the Second Drill Sergeant.

"Don't you do it, Santos," he growled. "Don't you quit on me now."

At that exact time, he felt nothing but the pain relief of the truck getting further away. His brain had turned off; the only thing working was instinct. Put one step in front of the other.

Lean forward. His legs felt like sticks propping him up. He didn't take the weight. He dragged him forward, forcing his legs to move. He turned to the recruit behind us.

"If he slows down," the Drill Sergeant roared, "you push him with your muzzle! Move!"

The threat cut through the fog. He entered a fugue state. *Left. Right. Left. Right.*

The pain, the raw meat of his feet, the fire in his lungs - it all faded into a white noise.

He didn't wake up until he saw the torches. They were flickering on the hill ahead, piercing the pre-dawn darkness like beacons. He crossed the line as the sky turned a bruised purple. He stopped. He didn't collapse.

He stood, swaying slightly, vibrating with exhaustion. We were the only platoon to finish without a single dropout.

At graduation, a Drill Sergeant joked to the families that if they had a member in 3rd platoon, their lives had been threatened to get them there. Everyone laughed. Except 3rd platoon. Our lives hadn't been threatened; they had been strengthened.

The Senior Drill Sergeant - the one with the Grenada lung - walked down the line. He stopped in front of him. He held up a small metal pin. The "Blood Rifles."

He didn't pin it gently. He punched it into his chest, driving the posts through the uniform and into the skin.

The sting was sharp. It was the best thing he had ever felt.

He wasn't the "Charity Kid" anymore. No one had given him this. He had paid for it in skin, breath, and bone.

As he left the field, he saw lines forming. Not for the PT studs, but for Sgt. Graves and Sgt. Jones. A line of recruits who couldn't wait to introduce their families to the men who had refused to let them fail.

CHAPTER 10
THE INHERITED WAR

August 2003 Midtown South, Manhattan NY

Santos came home in August, moved back into his apartment, and reported for his first drill with the unit in NYC.

The company formed up. First came the usual updates, and the introduction of four new soldiers fresh out of basic. A minute or two of "hooahs" and back-slapping followed, but then the formation quieted down.

The Company Commander stood before them, his face serious. Somber.

"Soldiers, the time has come," the CO said. "I received word from Albany that the 1/120th Infantry is being deployed, but they are at less than 50% strength. They have put out a statewide request for volunteers."

The air left the room.

"I stand here to remind you of your duty," he continued. "But your duty isn't only to the State or the Nation; it is to your family. If you find that duty is driving you to volunteer, do so. If it is driving you to hang back, there are plenty of rear detachment jobs. There is zero pressure, men. This is not Annual Training. This is the real deal. I cannot and will not pretend that if you volunteer, there isn't a chance you won't come home in a box. This is your choice and your choice alone."

He paused, looking down the ranks. "Take a minute to think about it. When I say move... if you volunteer, take one step forward."

Panic set in. Santos's heart hammered against his ribs. *What do I do? What is the answer?*

He looked straight ahead, paralyzed by the weight of the choice.

"MOVE!"

In that moment of indecision, something inside him took charge. He didn't consciously tell his leg to move. It just swung forward.

Thud.

The sound was singular. Massive.

He risked a glance to his left. Then to his right. The entire platoon had stepped forward. Not a single man had stayed back. They stood there, a new line formed in the concrete, bound by a terrifying and beautiful unity.

The CO looked at them, and Santos saw a tear track down his dust-covered cheek.

"I couldn't be prouder of you men."

Santos went home that weekend with the weight of the world on his shoulders. He made it to Wednesday.

He woke up that morning, staring at the ceiling, and the realization hit him like a physical blow: *I can't do this anymore.*

The spreadsheets, the commute, the "Grey Grind" - it was all meaningless ash in his mouth.

He picked up the phone and called his manager.

"I'm not coming in," he said.

"What do you mean?"

"I'm likely deploying to Iraq," he told him. "I just can't see myself staring at a screen when I only have a month before I leave for active duty."

He had some choice words for him. Santos didn't care.

He hung up the phone and sat in his kitchen with a cup of coffee, the silence of the apartment buzzing in his ears.

What the fuck did I just do?

He had no job. He had a war looming. He had a month to live a lifetime.

He drank the coffee. Then, he grabbed a notepad and started writing a bucket list.

The list didn't take long. The rest of the year dissolved into a blur of mobilization orders, gear layouts, and the freezing isolation of Fort Drum. They spent their final days in America shivering in the barracks, watching the snow pile up, waiting for the order to move.

When it finally came, they were ready to leave the cold behind, even if it meant walking into the fire.

January 2004 Kuwait / Iraq

The war didn't greet them with a bullet. It greeted them with a slap in the face.

Leaving Fort Drum, the world had been frozen in a state of suspended animation. The thermometer read fifteen degrees below zero, with a wind chill dragging it down past negative twenty. His blood had thickened, his body calibrated to survive the ice.

Then came the commute to hell.

It wasn't a tactical insertion. It was a surreal, two-day purgatory aboard a chartered civilian airliner. The plane was a wide-body beast - rows of two on the sides, three in the middle - filled not with tourists, but with hundreds of infantrymen clutching M4s between their knees.

He remembered grabbing his vest and putting it on, checking his gear in the middle of this beautiful, sterile cabin. It was an impossible contrast.

The flight attendants were young, attractive women. Seeing European women who looked like models was not something he saw in the Bronx that often. As they moved forward to board, it was all smiles - red lipstick and pearly white teeth.

But as he looked closer, something about the eyes and those smiles stood out to him. The smiles were forced. Some hid it really well, but on the rest, it looked like an invisible finger was pushing the corners of their lips up.

Then there were the eyes. They held their poise, but behind it was a distinct hint of fear.

He wondered if the fear was for the location or for the men themselves. He wondered how often these women, who were not much older than he was, saw groups of soldiers walk out of that aircraft with a blissful ignorance, only for another group to board a few hours later that looked like their souls had just touched the corners of hell.

The journey was a blur of sleeplessness and refueling stops. We touched down in Germany, then France, teasing them with glimpses of the civilized world through small oval windows before lifting off again toward the violence.

For forty-eight hours, they existed in that climate-controlled tube, suspended between the lives they were leaving and the war they were joining.

Then, the door opened in Kuwait.

The illusion of civilization vanished instantly. Reality hits at that moment. The sun was so bright it felt like a nuke had just gone off in front of his face. Equal to blizzard blindness, his eyes automatically started to tear up. It was like the Oakleys on his face were not even there; that sun didn't care about UV protection.

Camp Buehring was unforgiving - extremely light tanned sand that reflected the light like it was made of crushed glass.

The heat hit them like a physical wall. It was seventy degrees - technically mild compared to the Iraqi summer to come - but to bodies primed for the arctic winter of upstate New York, it felt like stepping into a blast furnace. The thermal shock was so violent it felt like the air had been sucked out of the lungs.

Across the tarmac sat a line of buses, but these were not the buses of the Bronx. These were Mercedes buses, painted white with dark tinted windows, and the trucks for their gear... those box trucks were like fancy U-Hauls.

The contradictions broke his brain. *Mercedes in the Middle East?*

He might have been twenty-two, but his knowledge of geography and world culture was sourly lacking. He thought the Middle East was a shit-hole filled with camels and thieves like something out of *Aladdin*. Why were these men in turbans and mustaches - the very people they were supposed to be ready to shoot - helping them with their bags?

Within the hour, they were on the move. It wasn't a long drive to the staging area, but the speeds these people drove were insane. In New York City, if you made it past forty or fifty miles per hour, you were cruising. He wouldn't be surprised if these drivers hit a hundred at some points.

When they reached their staging area, people had already started grabbing "under-the-truck" real estate. They found the nearest shady spot and crawled under. Camel spiders? *Don't care.* Scorpions? *Let them come.* Snakes? *Whatever.*

The only enemy they had at that moment was the sun.

His uniform was instantly heavy with sweat, and his body simply shut down, unable to compute the hundred-degree swing and the two days of travel.

He woke up two hours later. The sand was in his teeth. The war had begun.

The push north was a three-day convoy, a steel snake winding its way up the spine of the country. They weren't going to the massive, sprawling city-within-a-city at Balad Airbase, with its Burger King and internet cafes.

They were going to the outpost guarding its throat.

FOB Vanguard.

It sat about five miles southwest of the main airbase, a small, fortified pimple on the supply route.

They arrived in the golden haze of late afternoon. When they saw the bunkers, there actually seemed to be a sense of relief. They knew that it would take a massive strike to do significant damage or injury to those inside.

In the unlikely event of a rocket attack direct onto the doors, the enemy would have to have great aim and hit with multiple rounds to breach the steel and go against the mounted 240B on the top of the bunker - an Observation Post (OP) that was manned twenty-four hours a day, seven days a week.

This wasn't a war they had to build; it was a war they inherited, but they didn't inherit comfort.

The living quarters weren't tents. They were tombs. The Coalition forces had converted the old Iraqi ammunition depots into barracks. Massive, earth-covered concrete bunkers that had once stored artillery shells now stored men. They were cool, dark, and bomb-proof, but living inside them felt like living in a cave.

The infrastructure ended at the bunker door. Everything else was DIY.

It was either night one or night two that Santos got "shit burning detail." There were no tiled bathrooms. The latrines were plywood shacks raised over cut-out oil drums. Every day, the drums had to be pulled out, doused in diesel, and burned.

The black, oily smoke of burning waste became the signature scent of the FOB, a smell that stuck to the back of the throat and never left.

They had people who grew up in the suburbs - probably about seventy percent of the platoon. If the rock-bottom life was shocking to them, they didn't show it. Many of them were still blue-collar type individuals, handy men with skills. They looked at the primitive conditions not as a deficit, but as a project.

There were no showers - at least, not yet. They had to build them.

Using plywood and gravity-fed water bags, they constructed stalls that offered a trickle of lukewarm water. It was a return to the basics of survival that the "Charity Kid" recognized well.

It wasn't more than three nights before the suburban crew had expanded them from two or three showers to five or six. Others expanded on the latrines. And yet another group built a septic-type system to be able to use a salvaged washer that was there.

That first one failed within hours, flooding the area. That project was the tough one, but after a while, the engineers swung by and dug a decent-sized septic that had two stages: the initial holding right next to the bunker and then an overflow drain that flowed into a central pond area.

"Don't get comfortable," Sgt. Davis barked, though he looked just as relieved as the rest of them to be off the road.

They spent the first hour unloading trunks into the concrete gloom of the ammo bunkers. But before the sweat could dry, someone pulled out a disposable camera.

"Platoon photo," someone yelled. "Before we get ugly."

They gathered in front of their bunker. Santos stood shoulder-to-shoulder with Akin, adjusting his gear. They grinned, threw up hand signs, and flexed. They looked young. They looked invincible.

They looked like boys playing dress-up in heavy armor. It was the "Before" picture. The moment where everyone was present, everyone was whole, and the only scars they carried were the ones from the ruck march at Benning.

The honeymoon lasted a month. They settled into the rhythm of the rotation. Patrols. QRF. EOD security.

The boredom was the real enemy, a slow corrosion of alertness. The gunners had by now learned the little tricks. Pebbles for vehicles that got too close. Candy for the kids.

Then came the patrol south toward Taji.

It was a routine movement down Highway 1. His truck usually was the third in the stack of five or six trucks. So when it came to ambushes, his truck was probably the safest. Usually, the first truck was hit to create an obstacle, or the last truck would be hit to trap the convoy.

The drive was like every other drive up to that point. Boring.

He was in the back, watching the civilian traffic through the thick glass. The rules of the road were simple: locals gave way to the convoys.

But one car didn't.

A sedan trailing the convoy accelerated. It moved erratically, weaving out of the lane, pushing up aggressively on the rear vehicle's bumper.

"Watch that vehicle," the rear gunner called over the comms.

The sedan pulled alongside the rear truck. The window rolled down.

Probably a minute or so later came the first muffled thump of a grenade exploding. The asphalt kicked up debris.

Then the radio exploded with chatter: "Contact rear! Contact rear!"

The rhythmic sound of the .50 cal on the rear truck began to hammer.

The trucks herringbone out and took positions to maximize firepower. Team leader begins to give orders:

"Stanley, move rear. Santos, position at 12. Akin, cover the field."

And they started to move.

A second and third grenade had already exploded. He kicked his door open. The armored door weighed hundreds of pounds; he used the momentum of the stopping vehicle to swing it open, letting physics do the work.

He hit the dirt, weapon up, scanning his sector. They were returning fire - first from cover, then firing while maneuvering.

Taking a wedge position without a point man, the first two soldiers moved on the vehicle. Santos and Stanley, at the edge of the wedge, shifted from a forward firing position to a rear firing position in case there were insurgents that might hit from their flanks.

He could still smell the gunpowder coming off his rifle.

His breaths came in and out deeply - not hyperventilating, not in a panic. The breaths were deep, steady, and rhythmic. His body reacted to a life-threatening situation not with fear, but with automation.

It told his lungs to take in as much oxygen as possible. It told his sweat glands to provide a film of cooling sweat but retain fluid to prevent dehydration. His pupils were laser-focused.

Any function that wasn't needed for that moment was shut down, including his brain. In that moment, thinking wasn't necessary, only doing. To think was to not let your training kick in. So the brain takes five, while muscle memory says, "I got this."

The sedan had screeched to a halt, trying to turn around. Three men spilled out, AK-47s raised, firing wildly at the convoy.

Crack-crack-crack.

Rounds pinged off the Humvee's armor.

He didn't think about his mother, or the shelter, or the teacher from New Jersey. He thought about his sight picture. He thought about breathing.

The two fire teams opened up. It was a wall of disciplined violence. The .50 cal thundered in the background as it provided suppressive fire. M4s chattered in controlled bursts.

He squeezed the trigger. The recoil dug into his shoulder. He saw the dust kick up around the gunmen.

It was over in seconds. The three insurgents lay still on the road. The sedan was smoking metal and shattered glass.

"Cease fire! Cease fire!"

Silence rushed back in, ringing in their ears. They scanned for secondary devices, for a VBIED, for a follow-up attack. Nothing. Just the dead men and the heat.

"Status?" Sgt. Davis called out.

"Green," came the call from every team leader. "All Green."

They had been attacked. They had engaged. They had won. And nobody was bleeding.

He climbed back into the truck, his heart hammering against his ribs like a trapped bird. He looked at his hands. They weren't shaking. He looked at Akin across the cab. Akin nodded, a tight, grim smile on his face.

It was validation. The shouting at Benning, the pneumonia, the broken toes - it was all for this.

They weren't just kids in a photo anymore. They were warfighters.

As the smoke settled and the convoy prepared to move again, the realization took hold. The training worked.

They were untouchable.

CHAPTER 11
THE FLIES

Summer 2004 Dujail, Iraq

The air in Dujail didn't just sit; it pressed. It was a heavy, stagnant weight, flavored by the fine, talcum-like dust that found its way into every pore, every seam of the uniform, and every thought. To the world, Dujail was a dot on a map north of Baghdad. To the men of FOB Vanguard, it was the "City of Ghosts."

The history of the place was written in blood and ash. In 1982, Saddam Hussein's motorcade had been fired upon. In retaliation, his regime executed 148 men and boys, bulldozed the homes, and salted the earth by burning the ancient date palm orchards to the ground. The ghosts of those men still seemed to drift through the shadows of the replanted trees. The locals lived in a permanent state of guarded trauma. They didn't hate the Americans - not specifically - but they hated the violence that followed power.

The landscape was a high-stakes puzzle of "Friend, Victim, or Executioner." You could be handing a piece of candy to a child one second, and the next, a shadow in a second-story window was lining up a shot on your neck.

The call came in the dead of night.

It wasn't the radio that woke Santos. It was the earth. He was sleeping on a cot in the ammo bunker, the concrete floor acting as a conductor. A muffled thump vibrated through the foundation, a low-frequency pulse that hit his chest before it hit his ears.

Then came the distant, rhythmic *crack-crack-crack* of small arms fire.

"QRF! QRF! QRF!"

The radio screamed, but he was already vertical. In the Quick Reaction Force, the concept of "getting dressed" didn't exist. You slept in your boots. You slept in your uniform. You lived in a state of perpetual readiness that hammered your central nervous system into a jagged edge.

He grabbed his Interceptor body armor. The vest weighed nearly thirty pounds with the ceramic SAPI plates. He swung it over his head, the Velcro rasping like a saw as he cinched the side straps.

His heart rate, usually a steady drum, began to accelerate, a physiological redline. He could feel the adrenaline dumping into his bloodstream, a cold fire that sharpened the edges of the world. His pupils dilated, pulling in the dim light of the bunker. Every sound - the slap of a magazine into a well, the heavy breathing of the team, the grit of sand under his boots - was amplified.

We ran for the trucks.

The Humvee's engine was already roaring, a guttural, diesel growl that shook the chassis. He climbed into the back seat behind the driver. The interior smelled of stale sweat, CLP gun oil, and the dry, metallic scent of the air conditioning unit struggling against the Iraqi heat.

He checked his M4. One in the chamber. Safety on.

The heavy steel gate of FOB Vanguard rolled back with a screech of metal on metal. The convoy peeled out, tires screaming as they transitioned from the gravel of the base to the hard-packed asphalt of Highway 1.

THE CRACK

The drive was a blur of shadows and green-tinted night vision.

We hit the South Gate Extension, a notorious choke point. The road curved sharply here, forced to navigate between the high walls of a farmhouse and a dense treeline of date palms. It was an ambush hunter's dream.

He stared out the thick ballistic glass. The world outside was a silent movie of silhouettes. He was scanning the "fatal funnel," his eyes darting from the dark gaps between trees to the rooftops.

CRACK.

The sound was singular. Sharp. Like a whip snapping inches from his ear.

The movie slowed down. This is the physiological divergence of the combatant - the "Slo-Mo" effect. His brain began to process information at a rate the human body wasn't designed for.

He watched the window. In the center of the ballistic glass, a dime-sized impact crater appeared. From that center, a spiderweb of fractures blossomed with agonizing slowness. He watched the white lines of the shattered laminate reach out toward the edges of the frame. It looked like a frozen pond cracking under the weight of a stone.

The light from the dashboard caught the fractures, turning the window into a kaleidoscope of jagged geometry.

He stared at that dime-sized center. It was perfectly level with his throat.

Time dilated further. He could see himself from the outside - a soldier in a metal box, eyes glued to the point where a piece of lead had tried to end his story. Had they never received the up-armored kits? Had they been in the old canvas-sided Humvees?

The round would have transitioned through the air, through his neck, through the seat, and into the man behind him.

It would have been effortless.

In that fraction of a second, the man he was two minutes ago - the "Invincible Soldier" - evaporated. He didn't exist anymore. That version of Santos died against the glass.

What remained was something stripped of ego, something raw and mechanical.

He was sucked back into his body. The ringing in his ears snapped into the roar of the engine.

"Contact right!"

The driver slammed on the brakes. The Humvee's nose dived. The tires screeched, fighting for grip on the dusty pavement, sending a massive plume of grit over the windows. The vibration of the skid traveled through the floorboards and into his teeth.

"Time to move, Santos," he whispered to the void in his chest. "Get in the fight."

THE AMBUSH & VBIED

He reached for the door handle. The door of an up-armored Humvee weighs hundreds of pounds. It is a slab of steel and ceramic designed to stop an explosion. He didn't try to muscle it; he waited for the momentum of the truck's stop to swing it open.

As the vehicle lurched, he kicked the latch. The door swung wide with a heavy, metallic clunk.

He hit the dirt.

The ground was hot, even at night. The dust entered his lungs, tasting of minerals and spent gunpowder. He rolled into a kneeling position, his weapon up, tracking the treeline.

Muzzle flashes flickered in the orchard like lethal fireflies.

Thump-thump-thump-thump.

The .50 caliber machine gun on the roof roared to life. The sound was primal. It wasn't a "bang"; it was a physical percussion that hammered against his ribs, vibrating the very marrow of his bones. Every round sent a shockwave through the air that he could feel on his skin.

The tracers - bright red streaks of phosphorus - burned lines into the darkness, tearing through the grapevines and palms, turning wood into splinters and shadows into red mist.

Then, movement on the parallel dirt road. Headlights.

A truck was screaming toward them, kicking up a massive rooster tail of dust that hung in the air like a shroud. It was moving too fast for the terrain. It was a spear aimed at the heart of their convoy.

"Vehicle approaching! Seven o'clock!"

The gunner shifted. He fired a warning burst. Five rounds of .50 cal passed inches over the cab of the approaching truck. The tracers lit up the interior of the vehicle for a heartbeat.

Stop. Turn around. Give us a reason not to kill you.

The truck didn't slow. It accelerated. The engine screamed as the driver floored it, the vehicle bouncing violently over the ruts in the road.

In the adrenaline-soaked logic of an ambush, there is no "maybe." A vehicle ignoring warning shots and charging a line of soldiers is a VBIED - a Vehicle Borne Improvised Explosive Device.

A suicide bomber.

"Engage! Engage!"

The order was a release of tension. The entire line opened up. It was a wall of lead. He felt his M4 bucking against his shoulder, the rhythmic recoil a familiar, violent pulse.

He focused on the engine block, then the cab. The .50 cal rounds were punching holes the size of softballs through the metal.

The truck shuddered. The windshield vanished into a cloud of glass dust. The front tires blew out, the rims sparking against the rocks. The vehicle ground to a halt, steam and black smoke pouring from the shattered hood.

Just as the shooting from their line tapered off, the sky tore open.

The Apaches had arrived.

The sound of an Apache gunship engaging is unlike anything else on earth. It's been described as "ripping canvas," but it's deeper, more mechanical. It's the sound of a giant saw cutting through the atmosphere.

The two gunships dropped their noses, their 30mm cannons spitting high-explosive rounds into the orchard where the ambush fire had originated.

The treeline exploded. Dust, palm fronds, and debris were kicked thirty feet into the air. Two passes. That was all it took. The silence that followed was deafening. The shooting from the orchard didn't just slow down; it ceased to exist.

"Clear it," Sgt. Davis ordered.

THE TRUCK BED

He was point man on the driver's side. He approached the truck with his weapon at the high-ready, his finger resting lightly on the trigger guard. Every muscle was coiled. He expected the door to fly open. He expected a man with an AK-47 to tumble out, or the white-hot flash of a detonator.

He reached the driver's door. The glass was gone. The man behind the wheel was slumped over the steering wheel, a ruin of a human being. Multiple gunshot wounds to the head and chest. He wasn't a threat anymore. He was just meat and fabric.

Then, he heard it.

A soft, low moaning. It was coming from the back.

Training is supposed to make you a machine. It builds muscle memory until you can clear a room or a vehicle without thinking. It teaches you to be a killer, a weapon with a single mission: destroy the enemy.

But then, the Army hammers you with "Values." They tell you that we sit above the chaos because we cherish the sanctity of innocent life. We are taught to be wolves, but told to act like shepherds.

When those two worlds collide, the impact leaves a crater in your soul.

He walked toward the bed of the truck. Time didn't just slow down; it stopped. The green-tinted night vision felt like it was bleeding out, replaced by the stark, high-contrast horror of reality. The darkness of the Iraqi night encircled him, narrowing his world until the only thing that existed in the universe was the rusted metal of that truck bed.

The smells hit him first. They didn't come in sequence; they hit as a solid, suffocating wall.

It was a specific, industrial cocktail of death. The sharp, chemical sting of diesel fuel. The sickly-sweet, boiling scent of radiator fluid from the dying engine. The heavy, unmistakable copper tang of fresh blood. And beneath it all, the sharp ammonia of urine - the scent of a body losing control in its final moments.

It wasn't just human fluids. It was the bodily fluids of the machine they had just murdered. Oil, coolant, and exhaust from their idling Humvees swirled together with the blood, coating his tongue in a film he couldn't spit out.

His mouth went bone-dry. He raised his weapon over the rail of the truck bed.

His heart stopped.

There were no insurgents. There were no artillery shells wired to a cell phone.

Huddled in the corner of the bed was a woman in black robes. Her eyes were wide, fixed on him, reflecting the moonlight like shattered glass. In her arms, she clutched a little girl.

The girl was wearing pajamas. They were stained a deep, dark red. It wasn't the bright red of a spilled drink; it was the thick, viscous crimson of life leaving a small body. The mother's arm was wrapped around her, but the angle was all wrong - a bullet had shattered the bone, leaving the limb hanging in a sickening, impossible twist.

The girl moaned again.

In that moment, the "Automaton" died. The "Warrior" dissolved. All that was left was a human being standing on the edge of an abyss.

The void threatened to completely swallow him. It wanted him to drop his weapon and scream. But the survival instinct - the one forged in the Bronx, the one that survived the fire - clawed its way back.

I will not give up. I will not surrender. I didn't come all the way to this hellhole to get sucked into the black.

"Medic!" he screamed.

The word tore out of his throat, raw and jagged, shredding the silence. "Medic up! Now!"

The battle snapped back into focus. The sounds of the idling engines and the distant shout of orders rushed back in. He kept his weapon trained on the truck - doctrine demanded it - even as his heart was breaking.

We secured the scene. We did our job. But the damage was done. The "Noble Fight" had been shaken. We tell ourselves we are different because we don't try to harm the innocent, while the enemy seeks to. But looking at that little girl, the distinction felt like a lie.

That image didn't stay in Iraq. It followed him home. It waited for him to have children of his own.

He still has nightmares about that night. In the dream, he is yelling at the father and the grandfather. "You know you shouldn't come toward U.S. forces! We taught you that! Why would you drive at us? Why?"

But the dream shifts. The logic of the nightmare takes over.

He walks up to the truck bed in his sleep, the smell of diesel and blood choking him, and he looks over the rail.

It isn't an Iraqi woman anymore. It's his wife. She is looking up at him, terrified, her arm broken.

And in her arms, she isn't holding a stranger. She is holding his sons.

They are wearing their pajamas. They are bleeding out on the rusted metal. And they look at him - the man who is supposed to protect them, the man who pulled the trigger - and they moan.

"Daddy?"

It is the one dream that breaks him. It makes him wake up screaming in the dark of his home, his chest heaving, his face soaked in tears. He throws the covers off and runs down the hall to his boys' room.

He collapses on the floor between their beds, listening to the rhythm of their breathing, checking their chests to make sure they are rising and falling.

For those first few minutes, he is paralyzed. He is halfway between Dujail and Texas. He lays there on the carpet, begging God to take him instead of them. He pleads for that fraction of a second before his mind fully wakes up and realizes it was just a nightmare.

But even when he wakes up, the smell doesn't leave. The diesel. The copper. The rot. It fades back into the darkness of the closet, waiting. And so, he closes his eyes.

The medic pushed past him, his movements frantic. He checked the girl's pulse. He looked at the mother. He worked for maybe thirty seconds - thirty seconds that felt like thirty years.

Then he looked up. His face was gray in the moonlight. He shook his head.

"She's gone," he said quietly. "Nothing could have saved her. The .50 cal... it was over before it started."

Santos turned away. He couldn't look at the bundle in the woman's arms anymore. He needed to move. He needed to be a "Warrior" because being a "Human" was too much to bear.

He moved to the passenger side of the truck. That's where he found the grandfather.

The old man had been ejected from the cab when the truck hit the ditch. He was dressed in traditional white robes - a *dishdasha*. The contrast was horrific. The white fabric was now a canvas for the violence they had unleashed.

He had taken multiple 5.56 rounds to the chest, but the .50 cal - the "Thump-Thump" he had felt in his ribs - had hit him in the head.

He knelt beside him. The smell here was different. It was the sweet, rotten scent of exposed biological matter mixed with the copper.

He looked at his head. The skull was open. It wasn't a wound; it was an anatomy lesson. He could see the sinus cavity. He could see the gray folds of his brain. He could see the physical architecture of a lifetime of thoughts, memories, and prayers, spilled out onto the Iraqi dirt.

And then, he heard the buzzing.

In the few minutes since the shooting had stopped, the flies had found him. Hundreds of them. They were a black, roiling carpet over the wound. They swarmed the chunks of brain matter that lay in the dirt just inches from his knee.

The sound was a low, vibrating drone that seemed to drown out the idling Humvees and the hovering Apaches.

It was the sound of nature reclaiming a mistake. The flies didn't care about the "City of Ghosts." They didn't care about Saddam Hussein or the War on Terror. They didn't care about the rules of engagement or the "Noble Warrior." To them, this was just calories. This was just a resource.

"Hey, Santos."

Sgt. Davis was standing over him. He looked down at the grandfather, then back at him. He looked pale, his jaw tight.

"You don't need to look at this, man. Come on. Get back to the truck."

It was a kindness. It was the "Gray Beard" trying to protect the younger man from the images that never leave. But it was a useless gesture. The image was already burned into the back of his retinas. The white robes. The red earth. The black flies.

"I'm fine," he lied.

He wasn't fine. He was etching the scene into his DNA.

The Iraqi Security Forces (ISF) finally arrived, twenty minutes late. They moved with a lazy, disconnected indifference that made his blood boil. They began to collect the bodies, tossing them into the back of a flatbed like cordwood.

As we prepared to mount up, a group of civilians approached from the nearby farmhouses. A woman in black robes - the grandmother - broke from the group.

She wasn't wailing. She was screaming - a high, piercing sound that cut through the night air like a razor. As she got closer, her grief curdled into a visible, incandescent rage. She walked straight toward them, her hands hidden deep within the folds of her robes.

"Stop!" he yelled, bringing his M4 to his shoulder. "Stop! *Imshee!*"

She didn't stop.

Fifty meters. Forty.

The conditioning kicked in. The "Warrior" state took over, a cold, clinical bypass of his frontal lobe that prioritized ballistics over empathy. His heart rate, which had been a frantic gallop moments ago, leveled out into a flat, rhythmic pulse. He could feel the trigger - four pounds of resistance standing between life and a catastrophic mistake.

He had already applied three.

He squinted through the Trijicon optic. The chevron reticle glowed a faint, ghostly red, centered perfectly on the woman's chest. The magnification brought her too close. He saw the deep, weathered trenches of the wrinkles on her face, etched by decades of desert sun and sorrow. He saw the hate in her eyes - a pure, incandescent fury that didn't fear the rifle.

Then, the lens warped.

The heat rising from the road combined with the chemical spike in his brain, and the world began to liquefy. The sharp edges of the Humvee and the palm trees blurred into a static-filled haze. The black, dusty robes of the grandmother began to shift, the color bleeding out, replaced by the faded floral pattern of a worn housecoat.

The dusty Iraqi road didn't just change; it dissolved. He wasn't standing in the dirt of Dujail. He was standing on the cracked, yellowing linoleum of the Bronx apartment floor.

The smell of diesel and death was replaced by the cloying, suffocating scent of stale cigarettes and cheap floor wax.

It wasn't an Iraqi insurgent charging him. It was his mother.

She wasn't hiding a suicide vest in her robes. She was raising her right hand, and wrapped around her knuckles was the bright orange coil of an extension cord. He could hear the rhythmic *thwack-thwack-thwack* as she slapped the heavy rubber against her palm, testing the weight before the strike.

Her face was twisted into that familiar, unhinged mask of rage - the look that preceded the pain.

"You good for nothing and lazy!" she screamed.

The words didn't come from the desert air; they came from the humid, cramped hallways of his childhood. They were sharp, serrated blades cutting through the silence of the apartment. She wasn't a grieving grandmother; she was the judge and the executioner, coming to punish the very existence she resented.

He felt the phantom sting of the cord against his legs before she even reached him.

His finger tightened on the M4's trigger. The "Warrior" wanted to stop the threat. The "Child" just wanted to disappear.

He shook his head violently. The weight of the ACH helmet jarred against his temples, the chin strap digging into his throat.

Reset. Reset. Reset.

He blinked.

One.

The housecoat flickered, the floral pattern struggling against the black fabric of the robes.

Two.

The linoleum floor began to crack, the Iraqi sand pouring through the fissures.

Three.

Hard. He squeezed his eyes shut until he saw stars, then snapped them open.

The glitch cleared. The Bronx vanished into the ether. The desert returned with a sensory roar.

The woman was still coming, but the vision had settled back into the horrific reality of the present. She was twenty meters away now, her face a mask of agony, thrashing against the younger man who had rushed forward to catch her. He was pinning her arms, dragging her backward, his own face wet with tears.

The voice had changed. It wasn't the English of his childhood abuse anymore; it was the broken, guttural English of a woman who had seen her world decimated in a matter of seconds.

"Infidel you are, go!" she wailed, her voice cracking under the weight of her loss. She pointed a trembling finger at the truck, at the bodies, at the brass casings littering the road.

"My world, my life. NO, No NO."

He lowered the rifle. His hands were shaking so violently he had to grip the vertical foregrip until his knuckles turned white. The chevron reticle was gone, but the image of his mother with that orange cord remained burned into the periphery of his vision, a ghost lurking just behind the dust.

He climbed back into the Humvee and pulled the heavy door shut. He needed the steel. He needed the armor. He needed something - anything - to separate the man he was supposed to be from the boy he used to be.

But as they drove away from the screaming woman, he realized the armor only worked one way.

It kept the bullets out, but it did nothing to keep the ghosts in.

We drove back to the FOB in a silence so thick it felt like they were underwater. The validation of the ambush was gone. The "Warrior" identity felt heavy, like a suit of armor that was three sizes too small and rubbing his skin raw.

He realized then that the "Charity Kid" from his youth had it wrong. The worst thing in the world wasn't having nothing. The worst thing in the world was being the person who took everything from someone else.

He sat in the dark of the Humvee, his eyes trapped on the spiderweb crack in the window. It wasn't just damage; it was an existential reminder that the facade of the "Warrior" was fragile.

Two inches of ballistic glass was the only difference between being the person who delivered death and being the person who signed for its delivery.

In that moment, the duty and honor of the slogans - "An Army of One," "Be All You Can Be" - evaporated. They were marketing pitches for a job that dealt in meat and fluid. No matter how "high speed" an 11-Bravo is, eight grams of copper and lead moving at 2,900 feet per second doesn't care about your training.

If that glass hadn't held, he wouldn't have been a hero. He would have been the one who shit and pissed himself in the back seat. It would have been the copper smell of his blood imprinted on his squad's brains as they loaded his limp body into the back of their truck.

He waited for the morning. But when the sun rose from the horizon, it didn't bring a new day full of light. All the sun did that day was illuminate the darkness so that it was visible.

The "Invincible Platoon" was one step closer to the reality check of the year, but that night we had unlocked a different kind of achievement.

1st Platoon had achieved "Humble" status.

CHAPTER 12

THE INVINCIBLE PLATOON

October 2004 Near the Tigris River, Iraq

By October, they didn't just feel like soldiers. They felt like gods.

The platoon was on a streak that seemed to defy the laws of probability. They weren't just surviving the deployments; they were dominating them. They were fast, surgical, and untouchable. Command called it "Counter-Insurgency Operations." They called it "Projecting Power."

When their convoy rolled through a village, the atmospheric pressure shifted. The insurgents didn't just hide; they melted away, dissolving into the landscape rather than risk engaging them. The locals watched with a complex cocktail of emotions - awe, terror, and a grudging respect for the violence they kept on a leash. They had spent months kicking in doors, navigating complex ambushes, and snatching High-Value Targets (HVTs) without taking a single casualty.

Not a scratch.

They were the "Invincible Platoon." It was an intoxicating narrative. And that was the lie that nearly killed them all.

The raid on the compound that morning was the culmination of that arrogance. It had been perfect. Textbook.

They hit the objective at 0300, the darkest part of the night, moving under the green glow of night vision like wraiths. There was no shouting. No cowboy theatrics. Just the rhythmic breathing of men who knew their jobs better than they knew their wives.

They breached the outer gate not with a massive boom, but with a "whisper charge" - just enough explosive to cut the hinges without waking the neighborhood. They flowed into the courtyard like water.

The HVT - a mid-level financier who paid for the IED components killing kids in the next sector - never stood a chance.

They found him in his bed. He woke up to the blinding lumen of a SureFire tactical light and the cold muzzle of an M4 pressed against his cheek. He was zip-tied, hooded, and dragged out in his underwear before he could even rub the sleep from his eyes.

Total time on target: fourteen minutes. No shots fired.

As they prepped the convoy to head back to FOB Vanguard, the mood was electric. The adrenaline was starting to fade, replaced by the smug satisfaction of predators who had eaten well.

They secured the HVT in the back of Truck 2. They checked their weapons. They cracked jokes about breakfast.

They were winners.

Then came the call that shattered the illusion.

"Bravo Two-Six, this is Vanguard Base," the radio crackled. "Orders updated."

Sgt. Davis keyed the handset, wiping sweat from his forehead. "Send it, Vanguard."

"Return on Route Gold."

The air left the vehicle. Route Gold was the same hardball road they had used to ingress three hours ago. It was a cardinal rule of desert warfare, written in blood: Never go out the same way you came in.

Predictability is a death sentence. It gives the enemy time to adjust. It gives them a window to dig a hole, string a wire, and stack three 155mm artillery shells in the dirt.

Sgt. Davis gripped his radio handset so hard Santos thought the black plastic would snap in his hand. His jaw tightened, the muscles bunching.

"Negative, Six," Davis said, his voice dropping an octave. "Route Gold is likely compromised. We just drove down it. They know we're here. Requesting alternate extraction through the wadi to the east. Over."

There was a pause. A long, static-filled silence where they waited for sanity to prevail.

"Negative, Davis," the Battalion Commander's voice came back, clipped and annoyed. "Route Gold is cleared by ISR. The wadi is a risk for vehicle recovery if you get stuck. Take Gold. Move out."

The NCOs looked at each other. It was a look of pure, unadulterated frustration mixed with a creeping dread. The "Big Picture" guys in the air-conditioned Tactical Operations Center (TOC) were playing Chess on a digital map; they were the ones standing on the actual board, breathing the dust.

They were worried about a truck getting stuck in the mud; the platoon was worried about getting vaporized.

Davis stared at the handset for a second, wanting to spike it into the dirt. But he was a professional. He took a breath, swallowed the rage, and looked at his men.

"Mount up," Davis growled. "Keep your spacing tight. Eyes open."

Santos was exhausted. The adrenaline dump from the raid had left him hollow, scooped out from the inside. His legs felt heavy, like he was wading through wet concrete, as he staggered toward their vehicle, Truck 4. He was running on fumes, that dangerous twilight state between hyper-vigilance and passing out.

Up ahead, at Truck 3, he saw Akin. He was already climbing up the side of the vehicle, moving with an energy Santos couldn't fathom as he swung his legs toward the turret.

He paused halfway up, one boot on the armor, looking back at them with that signature grin. It was a smile that didn't belong in a combat zone - bright, mischievous, the kind that made the war feel like a temporary inconvenience they would laugh about over beers later.

"Let's get home, Santos," Akin shouted back at him, sliding his boots into the hatch of Truck 3. "Smooth ride back. I got top cover."

"See you at the gate, brother," Santos muttered, too tired to return the smile.

Thompson, his battle buddy, nudged him as they reached their truck.

"Hey, switch spots with me?" Thompson asked, shifting his gear. "I hate sitting behind the driver. No leg room."

Santos was too drained to care. "Sure."

He climbed into the back left seat, directly behind Spc. Stanley, their driver. Thompson took the other side.

The interior of the truck smelled like stale sweat, CLP gun oil, and dust. It should have been uncomfortable, but at that moment, it felt like a sanctuary.

Complacency is a creeper. It doesn't hit you all at once; it seduces you with comfort.

Santos did something he never did. He reached up and unbuckled the chinstrap of his ACH helmet. The heavy Kevlar felt like a vice on his temples. He pulled it off and set it on his lap, rubbing his sweaty hair.

He leaned his head against the cool, thick ballistic glass of the window. He just wanted to feel something that wasn't hot, sharp, or heavy.

He closed his eyes, listening to the diesel engine hum, trusting the armor, trusting the road, trusting the lie that they were untouchable.

We rolled out. The Invincible Platoon.

THE BELL

Santos didn't hear the explosion.

People think an IED is a loud "bang," like a firework or a gunshot. It's not. When it's close enough, sound doesn't have time to form. It's a physical presence. It's a mountain of sudden, atmospheric pressure that slams into the side of the truck, trying to occupy the same space as your body.

The world didn't go black. It turned white. A blinding, solid wall of white.

His head was thrown violently to the left, against the ballistic glass he had been resting on. There was no helmet to absorb the kinetic energy. His skull met the laminate with a sickening crack that vibrated down his spine.

Suddenly, he wasn't in a truck anymore. He was in a room full of bells.

A high-pitched, vibrating hum occupied every corner of his brain. It wasn't a sound he heard with his ears; it was a frequency that was vibrating his teeth. He tried to lift his hands, but they weren't there. He couldn't feel his arms. He couldn't feel his legs.

He was a floating ghost trapped in a vibrating metal box. *Movie Mode.*

Time fractured. The chaos of combat slowed down into a terrifying, frame-by-frame slide show.

He watched Spc. Stanley through a haze of gray smoke and suspended dust particles that floated in the air like snow. He was a hero in slow motion. Through the windshield, Santos saw that the truck in front of them - Truck 3 - had been hit hard.

It was a twisted wreck of flaming metal, slewed sideways and blocking the kill zone.

Stanley didn't panic. In the silence of Santos's own head, he watched the driver's muscles tense. Stanley gripped the steering wheel, his knuckles turning bone-white. He didn't hit the brakes. He slammed the accelerator.

Santos felt the lurch as he rammed their Humvee into the burning carcass of Truck 3. Metal screamed against metal - a vibration he felt in his feet but couldn't hear.

Stanley used their momentum to shove the wreckage out of the way, clearing the kill zone for the rest of the convoy.

Santos could see his mouth moving, wide open, the cords in his neck standing out. He was screaming something, a primal roar of effort and fear, but the bells in Santos's head drowned him out.

It was a silent movie of survival.

His eyes drifted forward, through their windshield to the gunner's hatch of the truck in front of them. The turret should have been spinning. The .50 caliber machine gun should have been firing.

He waited for the visual of Akin laying down hate, keeping them safe.

It never came. The turret of Truck 3 was still.

Then, they drove past the site of the blast.

Santos looked out the window, his cheek sliding against the glass that had cracked his head. The smoke cleared for a split second, framing the scene like a photograph.

He saw the crater - a black scar in the earth. He saw the medic.

He was kneeling in the dirt, frantic, his hands buried deep in the chest of a soldier who had been thrown clear of the turret.

It was Akin.

The realization hit Santos harder than the blast. The "Invincible Platoon" was gone.

The bells kept ringing, indifferent to the fact that his world had just ended.

The "Bells" stopped. The high-pitched hum was replaced by a low, guttural roar that started in his gut and traveled to his throat.

The "Invincible Platoon" was a lie. The false idol of 1st Platoon was dead, and one of his brothers, one of only a couple who he called friend, was being held together by a medic's desperate fingers.

The rage didn't just wake him up; it set him on fire.

THE WHEAT FIELD

"DISMOUNT! DISMOUNT!"

Sgt. Davis's voice broke through the ringing in Santos's head. It wasn't a sound; it was a vibration that rattled his teeth.

He fumbled for the door handle. His fingers felt numb, like sausages, but muscle memory took over. He kicked the armored heavy door open and spilled out onto the hard-packed dirt of Route Gold.

He expected pain. He expected to feel the cracked skull or the bruised ribs. But he didn't feel anything.

He didn't feel the concussion that was currently scrambling his equilibrium. He didn't feel the heat of the Iraqi morning.

He only felt lava. A thick, molten rage bubbling up from his stomach, filling the empty space where the fear should have been.

He grabbed his M4 carbine, charging the handle with a violence that almost jammed the bolt.

To the right of the road, stretching out toward the Tigris, was a vast, golden wheat field. The stalks were high, waist-deep, swaying gently in the breeze as if the world hadn't just ended.

That's where the trigger-man was. That's where the wire led. That's where the cowards were hiding.

"Line formation!" Davis ordered, his voice cracking. "Sweep the field! Push!"

There was no hesitation. No one waited for a second command. They didn't check for cover. They didn't look for defilade. They simply formed a line abreast, spaced five meters apart.

They moved into the wheat field like a scythe. They were a line of steel and hate, moving with a cold, mechanical precision that was terrifying to behold.

This wasn't a "Noble Fight" anymore. This wasn't about winning hearts and minds. This was an execution.

They saw them. Four of them.

They were trying to crawl through the wheat toward a dry irrigation ditch about a hundred meters out. They were frantic. They were sloppy. They were thrashing through the dry stalks, thinking the gold would hide them.

"Contact!"

The shout rippled down the line.

They didn't hit the dirt. They didn't yell for surrender. They didn't follow the Rules of Engagement card tucked in their pockets.

The line just stepped forward, weapons shouldered, eyes locked on the movement.

Pop. Pop. Pop.

The M4s barked in a synchronized rhythm. It wasn't the chaotic spray of panic fire. It was professional. It was disciplined. It was the sound of a machine doing exactly what it was designed to do.

They watched the wheat stalks shatter as the rounds cut through them. They saw the dust puffs kick up around the crawling figures. They watched them jerk, spasm, and then go still.

One of them was still moving.

Santos broke the line. He walked forward, his boots crushing the wheat. The ringing in his ears was deafening now, a scream that matched the one inside his head.

He walked up to the last insurgent. He was curled in a fetal position, his hands clutched over his head, sobbing into the dirt.

He was young. He was terrified.

Santos didn't see a human being. He didn't see a political combatant. He looked at him and saw the empty turret of Truck 3. He saw the reason Akin was in the dirt. He saw the reason his head felt like it was splitting open.

He stood over him, his shadow falling across his face.

He raised his rifle, the holographic sight settling on his head.

His finger took up the slack on the trigger, feeling the wall before the break.

He wanted to see the life leave his eyes. He wanted to reclaim the power the IED had stolen from them. He wanted to balance the cosmic scale. One for one.

"SANTOS! BACK TO THE TRUCKS!"

The voice was a whip crack. Sgt. Davis didn't just yell; he projected command authority. It cut through the red haze, pulling Santos back from the edge of a cliff he couldn't climb back up.

He froze. The trigger was right there. Just four pounds of pressure.

"STAND DOWN, SANTOS!"

He lowered the rifle, the barrel shaking violently. His chest heaved, gasping for air that felt too thin. He tasted copper - he had bitten through his tongue in the blast and hadn't even realized it.

He looked down at the man in the dirt one last time, then turned his back.

They walked back to the convoy. The wheat field was silent again, save for the rustle of the wind.

He reached their Humvee. The medic was there, packing up his kit. His hands were covered in bright, arterial red. He was wiping them on his pants, but the stain wouldn't come out. He didn't look at Santos. He didn't have to.

"He's gone, Santos," Stanley whispered. He was leaning against the hood of the truck, his helmet off, shaking uncontrollably. "Akin is gone."

Santos turned toward Truck 2. The HVT - the man they had raided the compound for, the prize - was sitting in the back, hooded and silent.

He was alive. He was safe. He was going to get three meals a day, a lawyer, and a trial.

Akin was in a black vinyl bag.

The injustice of it hit Santos like a second blast.

He lunged for the door of Truck 2, his hand reaching for the 9mm pistol on his thigh. He was going to finish the cycle.

"SANTOS! STOP!"

Sgt. Davis hit him like a linebacker. He tackled him into the side of the armored door, pinning him against the steel. He was older, tired, but at that moment, he was a wall of granite.

He held him there, his forearm against his chest, until the fight drained out of his limbs.

"Not like this," Davis hissed in his ear, his face inches from his. "We are not them. You hear me? We are NOT them."

Santos slumped against the steel, the energy leaving him all at once. The adrenaline crash was brutal. His head throbbed with every heartbeat, a sledgehammer against the inside of his skull.

The "Invincible Platoon" was gone. They weren't gods. They weren't untouchable. They were just broken men, covered in the dust of a country that didn't want them, waiting for the next bell to ring.

He looked at the spot in the back seat where he had sat - the spot where he should have been wearing his helmet - and realized that the only thing thinner than the ballistic glass was the line between life and the dirt.

Akin had taken the hit. And he was still here.

The calendar kept turning after that day in the wheat field. October bled into November, and the missions continued. They still geared up, they still went outside the wire, and they executed every objective with lethal proficiency.

But the war - the real war inside them - had ended the moment the smoke cleared on Route Gold. They didn't fight because they felt like they were winning anymore, and they certainly didn't fight to "Project Power."

They fought because they refused to lose anyone else. Akin had paid the bill; the tab was closed.

The memorial service came and went, his face was painted onto the concrete T-walls of the FOB, and they drank cheap, illicit hooch in his honor under the desert stars.

As for the Battalion Commander, he retreated into the air-conditioned fortress of Headquarters. They never heard an apology, and they never openly spoke a word of insubordination against him. They didn't have to.

The silence was loud enough. He had made the call against SOP, against the pleas of the NCOs, and he knew it. It was a fatal mistake, a tactical error that cost a life, but it was his cross to carry now, just as heavy as the one they bore.

They finished their time in that country not as the "Invincible Platoon," but as a family bound by a single, ironclad promise: We were getting the rest of us home.

CHAPTER 13
THE EMPTY GYM

February 2005 – Fort Drum, New York

There is a distinct line where the war ends and the rest of your life begins, but it isn't drawn on a map. It's drawn in the quiet moments that follow the chaos.

If the blast on Route Gold was the violent finale of their innocence, the return home was the somber opening of their reality. The curtain had fallen on the "Invincible Platoon," and after a long, disorienting intermission, it rose again on a stage that felt too big, too empty, and terrifyingly quiet.

The war didn't end with a bang; it ended with a checklist.

Demobilization was a bureaucratic stripping away of the self. For a year, Santos had been a part of a machine. He had worn forty pounds of ceramic and Kevlar that defined his silhouette. He had carried a weapon that defined his power. Now, piece by piece, he handed it back.

The armor went into a bin. The M4 went into a rack. The sensitive items were counted and signed for. With every item he surrendered, he felt lighter, but also less substantial. Without the gear, he was just a twenty-four-year-old guy in desert fatigues that were already starting to feel like a costume.

It was more than just plastic and canvas. For the last year, the Army had been his father, his mother, and his god.

It had dictated his caloric intake, his sleep cycle, and his moral compass. He had lived in a world of absolute binary: Safe or Unsafe. Friend or Foe. Alive or Dead.

As he handed the Supply Sergeant his canteen cup - the metal dented from where he'd banged it against a rock in Samarra - he realized he was handing back his purpose.

There was no manual for what came next. In the military, incompetence gets you killed; in the civilian world, incompetence just makes you invisible. He was about to walk out into a world where no one would tell him where to stand, and for a kid who had spent his life looking for a system to belong to, that freedom felt a lot like falling.

Then came the ceremony.

The battalion gathered in the main gymnasium. It was a cavernous space, smelling of floor wax and sweat. The bleachers were packed with families - wives holding babies who had been born while their fathers were patrolling Highway 1, mothers clutching American flags, fathers beaming with pride.

The noise of anticipation was a physical hum in the air.

The speeches were long. Officers spoke about honor, about sacrifice, about the job well done.

Santos stood in formation, staring straight ahead. He didn't look at the bleachers. He didn't scan the crowd.

He already knew.

"Dismissed!"

The command broke the spell. The formation dissolved. The discipline of the Infantry evaporated as hundreds of soldiers turned toward the stands.

The families flooded the floor. It was a tidal wave of reunions - screams of joy, tears, the collision of bodies hugging.

Santos stood still. The tide rushed around him, breaking against him like water around a rock. He saw his squadmates disappear into the arms of their people. He looked at the empty space in the formation where Akin should have been standing.

There was no reunion for him, and there was no reunion for Santos.

He stood alone in the center of the gym. He checked his watch. He adjusted his cover. He waited for a few minutes, just to be sure, but he wasn't waiting for a person; he was waiting for the clock to run out on the formality.

It felt familiar. It felt like the escalator.

The memory hit him hard, pulling him back to the R&R trip months earlier.

He had flown home for two weeks of leave in the middle of the deployment. He had landed at LaGuardia, the gateway to the city he had gone to war to protect. He had one carry-on backpack. No checked bags. He walked out of the gate, bypassing the baggage claim carousel, heading straight for the exit.

He reached the top of the escalator. He took a deep breath. It felt like hope, but deep down, it was just the muscle memory of disappointment preparing to fire.

Down.

As the escalator descended, the reception area came into view. It was crowded with people holding signs, drivers searching for fares, and families waiting for loved ones. He scanned them. He looked left. He looked right. He scanned every face in the crowd.

Not one was familiar.

A slight, crooked smile formed on his face. It wasn't happiness. It wasn't relief. It was the dark satisfaction of a hypothesis confirmed.

The "Charity Kid" inside him whispered: See? I told you.

As he reached the bottom, the feeling of being alone returned like a heavy coat he had briefly taken off. He had a destination. There were people all around him, bumping shoulders, dragging luggage. But they weren't real. They were just Non-Player Characters in a one-player game. He was moving through a simulation where he was the only sentient thing.

He stepped off the escalator, did one final, perfunctory scan of the room, and walked to the phone banks.

He dialed the number. He watched the crowd as it rang.

"Hello?"

"Hi," he said. "I'm at LaGuardia. I guess no one is here?"

"No," the voice on the other end said, confused. "We were there yesterday. We waited for hours. We asked about your flight number and they said it wasn't arriving until today."

"Oh," he said. "Okay. Well, I'll be home in a bit. I'll grab a cab."

He hung up. He didn't argue. He didn't point out that he had given them the correct date, the correct flight, the correct time.

It didn't matter. The result was the same.

He walked out to the curb and hailed a taxi. He threw his bag in the back and climbed in.

Hello, old friend, he thought, greeting the solitude.

He rode in the back of the cab, staring out at the grey highway, sinking deeper and deeper into the black hole that was his world. The cab driver asked him a question; he gave a hollow answer.

He was back in the city of millions, entirely alone.

Back in the gym at Fort Drum, the crowd was thinning out.

The reunions were moving to the parking lot, to the cars, to the steakhouses and the hotels. Santos picked up his duffel bag. There was no phone call to make this time. He knew the drill.

He caught a ride with Thompson, who was driving his beat-up Ford pickup back to New Jersey. He offered to drop Santos in the Bronx on his way down.

Two hours outside the gate, they stopped at a travel plaza on I-87. The civilian world announced itself not with a bang, but with a neon sign for Dunkin' Donuts.

"Grab me a Gatorade?" Thompson asked, pumping gas.

"Sure."

He walked inside. The automatic doors slid open with a cheerful whoosh, blasting him with air conditioning that smelled of stale coffee and floor cleaner.

He walked to the cooler in the back. He reached for the handle and froze.

In the Army, you drink water. Sometimes, if you're lucky, you get a warm Rip It energy drink or a pouch of electrolyte powder. That was it. Binary choices.

Here, there were fifty different colors of liquid. Vitamin Water. Gatorade. Powerade. SoBe. Red. Blue. Yellow. Frost. Fierce. Zero Sugar. Recovery. Energy.

He stood there, his hand hovering over the glass, staring at the rows of plastic bottles. My brain, wired for scanning sectors and identifying threats, tried to process the tactical advantage of 'Blueberry Pomegranate' versus 'Fruit Punch.'

There was none. It was just noise.

The condensation on the glass blurred his reflection. He looked like a ghost haunting a convenience store.

"Hey buddy, you buying or browsing?"

A heavy-set man in a Giants jersey was standing behind him, holding a bag of chips. He wasn't being mean; he was just being a New Yorker. He was in a rush. He had places to be.

Santos flinched. The sudden voice behind him sent a spike of adrenaline through his chest that was entirely disproportionate to the situation. His hand went to his hip, reaching for a weapon that wasn't there.

"Sorry," he mumbled.

He grabbed the first red bottle he saw and walked away, his heart hammering against his ribs. He paid with a crumbled ten-dollar bill, not waiting for the change.

He walked back to the truck, the bottle sweating in his hand. He felt foolish. He had just survived a year of combat, but he had almost had a panic attack picking out a beverage.

"You good?" Thompson asked as he climbed in.

"Yeah," he lied. "Just tired."

He realized then that the hardest part of coming home wasn't going to be the big things. It was going to be the small ones. The world was loud, bright, and demanding, and he had forgotten the language.

A center console separated Thompson and Santos, but it might as well have been a dimensional rift. Outside the window, New York City was screaming with life.

He saw a man in a suit yelling into a cell phone because a light turned red. He saw a couple arguing over where to eat lunch. They were playing a game with no stakes. They were sleepwalking through a luxury they didn't even know they had: the luxury of boredom.

He stared at them, trying to remember how to be one of them.

How do you care about a traffic jam when you know what burning diesel and seared flesh smell like?

He had no reference point. His biological father was a ghost; his stepfather was a memory; and his Drill Sergeants were a thousand miles away. He was an alien in the passenger seat of a beat-up Ford, studying the humans, wondering if he could ever mimic their movements well enough to pass as one of them.

Thompson pulled the truck up to the curb and double-parked in front of his mother's building.

What should have been an impatient excitement to see his family was a dead stare out of the windshield. It wasn't a stare of observance. It was a stare that ended with the realization that he had accomplished something only one other distant relative in his family had.

A half-uncle on his father's side was a Marine who had deployed to Vietnam. His other uncle, the sole positive male figure in his life, was in the Marines, but he did not go to combat.

He was officially a combat veteran. He had the Combat Infantryman Badge (CIB). No physical scars other than a small mark on the back of his head from hitting a deuce-and-a-half truck. The internal wounds were festering and ready to take hold, but they hadn't been revealed yet.

The medals were in his bag, but his chest did not swell with pride.

No, he sat in that passenger seat, realizing the full circle was here. He wasn't only "back home," he was back at his mother's home.

Thompson knew. His face betrayed him, but he spared him the pity of the moment.

We got out, and as he helped Santos with his bags, he began with the pleasantries. They had spent a year arguing on a thirty-day rotation over who got the top bunk versus the bottom bunk. They had pulled security for each other when they had to dig a hole so they could drop one in the middle of nowhere.

It was Thompson who had ripped the bottom half of his undershirt to pass to Santos when they were on a mission and he forgot some TP. There was a bond between them that only those who shared the same experiences understood.

But in that moment, they felt like strangers.

"Alright man, take care," Santos said. "Make sure you call me when you get home."

He didn't. And Santos honestly didn't expect it.

Thompson replied, "Yeah man, you take care too. If you need anything just hit me up. See you at drill next month."

We gave each other a strong hug, probably the only genuine part of the whole interaction. We were two men lost, their Command having released them back to their civilian lives but never instructing them how to be civilians.

The difference between them was that Thompson had a wife to go home to. He had a teenage kid at home. He had purpose; he might not have seen it in that moment, but he had gravity pulling him back down to life.

Santos didn't have that. He had a mother who smiled as if she didn't spend the majority of his childhood yelling at him, telling him how worthless he was or throwing whatever object would hurt the most. Or a father who pretended that he didn't spend a chunk of his childhood treating him like a convenient object to satisfy his sick desires.

Civilian Thompson and Civilian Santos didn't know each other, and thus the battle buddies embraced that final time.

As they turned and stepped away into their civilian lives, Specialist Thompson and Specialist Santos faded into the deep recesses of dormancy, replaced by Lewis and the man he used to be.

Santos threw his duffle on his back, looked at his ruck, his second duffle, and finally his black trunk. He dropped the first duffle and enlisted Santos one last time to get his ruck and two duffles on his back.

I'll be damned if I ask anyone for help.

He humped it up the stairs and into the apartment. His cousin's husband offered his assistance, but he denied it. He dropped the bags and headed back down for the trunk.

One last look at the road. Thompson was long gone.

Alright Santos, he thought. You got this. Put the mask on, smile, and just suck it up. You don't have a choice, so deal with it.

He hauled the trunk up the stairs, the last trip in. He dropped it in the hallway and looked around for the first time.

He saw the sign: "Welcome Home."

He smiled and thanked everyone, but internally he thought about how nice this would have been this morning at the actual family reunion ceremony.

Then, immediately, the correction came: Quit pitying yourself.

"We got some t-bones and yuca fries," his cousin's husband said, clapping him on the shoulder.

"Thanks, that sounds good," Santos said. "Got any Coors?"

"Nah man, we didn't get any. I think Titi doesn't want you to drink."

And so it begins.

His aunt and cousin, the keepers of morals and the judges of all, were already trying to control the situation and, by default, him.

"Alright, I will be back," he said, turning to the door. "You want anything from the store?"

"Nah, how about we keep it cool today?" he said.

"No, I could use a drink, man. It's been a long day and a cold one will do me good."

"Alright man, but Titi is going to be a bit upset."

"Why?" he asked, stopping. "What is a beer going to do that is going to upset her? It's been six months since I have been eight months since I had a beer."

"Can I enjoy a fucking cold one?" he snapped. "Don't you think I have earned some respect to not need the approval from you guys to do something?"

"Yeah man, I am just saying she mentioned it because she doesn't want any trouble."

"What trouble does she expect?"

In that moment, he realized that absolutely nothing has changed.

He stood there, the same little kid that everyone saw, the one who was always treated as the problem. As long as he was the problem, they didn't need to look inward at themselves to see the imperfections within their own souls.

So the battle began. Not with them, but within himself. It was the battle between who he knew he could be, and the person everyone forced him to be.

He walked into his old bedroom and closed the door. The silence that followed wasn't peaceful; it was the silence of a truce that wouldn't last.

He knelt beside the green canvas bag and slowly pulled the zipper. The sound was aggressive in the quiet room, like a zipper tearing open a wound. Immediately, the smell hit him. It was the distinct perfume of the deployment - a mixture of burning trash, diesel fuel, and ancient dust that had baked into the fabric. It wafted up, instantly fighting with the smell of lavender potpourri.

He reached in and pulled out a handful of items, laying them out on the faded blue carpet. There was a jagged piece of shrapnel he'd picked up near the Tigris. There was a stack of Iraqi dinar notes with Saddam's face on them. There was a letter he had started writing to Thompson but never finished.

These were the artifacts of his reality. In the barracks, they were just clutter. Here, in this room preserved from his high school years, they looked violent and ugly. They were intrusive, like muddy boots on a white wedding dress.

He realized then that there was no safety net here. There was no wisdom waiting for him in this house. If he was going to survive the peace, he couldn't wait for someone to give him permission to be okay.

That was the lesson. The Army had taught him to clear a room; life was now teaching him that he had to build the house.

He was the only one who could stop the bleeding.

And as the silence of the house closed in, the only question that mattered remained: Was the wound fatal?

CHAPTER 14
THE BLACKOUT

Spring 2005 The Bronx, New York

The most dangerous thing in the world for a soldier without a war is a bank account full of deployment money and nothing to do.

Santos had spent a year in the desert where every minute was accounted for. Every movement was tracked. Every dollar he earned was deposited into an account he couldn't touch because there was nowhere to spend it. He came home with a small fortune by Bronx standards - thousands of dollars of "Hazard Pay" and "Combat Pay" sitting there, waiting.

It was supposed to be the seed money for a new life. Instead, it became the fuel for a fire.

The slide wasn't dramatic at first. It looked like celebration. He was twenty-four, he was alive, and he had cash. The script said: *Time to party.*

He hit the clubs. It was a sensory assault - bass thumping in his chest like a .50 cal, strobe lights mimicking muzzle flashes. He bought rounds for friends, for strangers, for anyone who would stand near him. He surrounded himself with noise and bodies, trying to recreate the density of the platoon.

But the "Alone Mentality" he had picked up at the airport didn't vanish when the music started. He would stand in the middle of a crowded dance floor, holding a twenty-dollar drink, watching the civilians laugh and grind. They were soft. They were oblivious. They were NPCs in a game he had already beaten.

The alcohol was a social camouflage. If he held a drink, he looked like he belonged. If he was drunk, the silence in his head - the space where Akin's jokes or Sgt. Davis's orders used to be - didn't echo as loudly.

Then, the sun would come up. The clubs would close. And Santos would have to go back to his mother's house.

That's when the drinking changed.

It stopped being social. It became medicinal.

The nights in the Bronx were quiet, but Santos's brain was loud. The TBI from the IED had left him with a low-level hum, a ringing bell that got louder when the world got quiet. Memories of the flies in Dujail or the smell of the burning truck would loop on the back of his eyelids.

He found the off switch in a bottle.

It went from a few beers to a few shots. Then it was a nightly ritual: drink until the brain shuts down. Drink until the bells stop ringing. Drink until the "Warrior" passes out so the "Charity Kid" doesn't have to think about the future.

The weeks blurred. Days were spent in a hungover fog, waiting for the night so he could disappear again. He was burning through his savings, burning through his liver, and burning through the goodwill of the universe.

He tried to play the game. He really did.

He put on a suit - one that felt too loose after the weight loss of the deployment - and walked out into a city that theoretically wanted to help him.

The narrative on the street in 2005 was that heroes were welcome. Support for the troops was at an all-time high. Yellow ribbons were on every bumper, and companies were bending over backwards to hire veterans. It felt like if you had a DD-214, you had a golden ticket.

But the golden ticket only works if there is a train to catch.

He went back to what he knew: money. He applied to banks, check-cashing stores, and currency exchange offices. He knew the systems. He knew the counts. He had the experience to run a branch in his sleep.

The problem wasn't his skills; it was his history. The major player in the New York currency game was the firm he had abandoned with a phone call a month before deploying.

He had burned that bridge to the waterline. That door was welded shut.

The only other options were the smaller firms operating out of JFK and LaGuardia, but those spots were dead man's shoes - no one left them, and openings were rare.

He looked at the rest of the landscape. The financial industry was still limping from the aftershocks of 9/11. Consumer sentiment was low. The city felt economically bruised. The only people making real money were the defense contractors and the real estate moguls.

He thought about contracting - going back to the sandbox for triple the pay - but he was still under contract with the Army until 2008. He couldn't double-dip. As for real estate? He didn't know the first thing about selling a condo, and he didn't have the patience to learn.

So he kept circling the same drain. He applied for the same teller jobs he was overqualified for, waiting for callbacks that never came because the industry was shrinking, not growing.

He wasn't being rejected because he was a soldier; he was being rejected because he was a dinosaur in a dying sector.

He sat in his mother's house, a specialized tool with no war to fight and no money to count. That was the day the bottle stopped looking like a party and started looking like a solution.

He was spiraling. But he wasn't blind.

One morning, waking up with another headache, looking at the same ceiling in the same room he had lived in as a child, he felt a sudden, profound exhaustion.

It wasn't physical tiredness; it was spiritual fatigue.

This is tiresome, he thought.

The scene - the drunkenness, the hangovers, the waste - felt pathetic. It lacked dignity. The Drill Sergeant with one lung wouldn't live like this. Akin didn't die so Santos could drown in vodka.

He didn't go to rehab. He didn't call a therapist.

He did what he had learned to do at Benning: he looked for a mission.

He found it in a listing for State Active Duty. The Department of Homeland Security needed National Guard soldiers to protect critical infrastructure. Specifically, the Indian Point Nuclear Power Plant just north of the city.

It was a return to the uniform. It was armed security. It was high stakes. It was Structure.

Santos put in his packet. He cleaned up. He shaved the depression beard.

He put the uniform back on, and as he fastened the buttons, he felt the pieces of himself clicking back into place.

The drinking stopped. Not because he was forced to, but because a soldier on duty doesn't drink. The mission required clarity, so he provided it. He was his own intervention.

He reported for duty at Indian Point. Standing guard towers, checking perimeters, operating within a chain of command - it was the antidote to the chaos. The bells in his head quieted down, not because of alcohol, but because they were drowned out by the familiar rhythm of duty.

The routine became the medication. The schedule was predictable - twelve on, twelve off. Four days on, three days off. The "on" days were a grind, leaving just enough time to eat, do laundry, catch a movie, and pass out before the alarm went off again.

But the "off" days? They were the reward.

The State paid for their lodging at a travel hotel nearby. In the summer, the single guys - the ones like him with no family tethering them home - turned the hotel into their own FOB.

They hit the pool. They hit the gym. They took the Metro North down to the city to walk Times Square or grab lunch, moving through the crowds like tourists in their own hometown.

Financially, he was bulletproof. Room and board were paid for. He had meal tickets for the hotel restaurant - where the Lobster Bisque bread bowls became a staple of his diet. Aside from a cell phone bill, a car payment, and insurance, every dollar he earned stayed in his pocket.

They rotated through the stations to keep the edge sharp.

At the Front Gate, they provided the overwatch while private security searched the vehicles. On Interior Patrol, they navigated the maze of industrial steel. At the OP, they watched the Hudson from the cliffs. And on the Boat - a converted Coast Guard vessel manned by Vietnam-era Navy vets - they acted as the rapid response force on the water.

People often asked if it felt weird to be fully armed in New York, standing guard in full battle rattle while civilians drove past in Toyotas. They asked if they were bored.

The answer to both was no.

They weren't bored because they knew the stakes. They viewed the mission as a direct extension of the Global War on Terror. They weren't there to catch shoplifters; they were a show of force.

They knew that just by standing there, by looking professional and lethal, they were hardening the target. The data proved it - attacks on sites with a Guard presence dropped to zero. They were the deterrent.

And the civilians? They didn't look at them like they were crazy. They looked at them like they were necessary.

The area around the plant was deeply conservative, a massive contrast to the city he had grown up in. It was his first real run-in with that side of America. People were polite. They waved. They thanked them. They bought them coffee.

In the Bronx, a uniform could make you a target or a curiosity. Here, it made you part of the community.

For a year, he lived in this bubble of respect and structure. He was fit, he was flush with cash, and he was respected. It was the perfect decompression chamber.

But as the months ticked by, he knew the contract had an expiration date. The ice he was standing on was comfortable, but it was thin.

If he wanted to stay out of the dark water, he needed to keep moving. He needed a new objective.

During a trip to visit friends at Fort Hood, Texas, he found two.

The first was a state with a booming economy and a cheap cost of living - a place where a man could build a fortress of his own.

The second was a girl. Vanessa.

She had just graduated with her BA, wide-eyed and eager to make waves in an industry he despised. Her world was built on celebrities, materialism, and drama - a shallow pool where success was based on who you knew, not what you did.

The statistical probability of her "making it" was near zero, but to him, her carefree delusion was refreshing. It was a window into the world he had only seen on TV, a world where the biggest problem was a wardrobe malfunction, not an IED.

They started talking about the future. His tactical map originally pointed to Orlando. He had two cousins there who had built good lives; the cost of living was low, and the weather was decent. It was the safe play.

But Vanessa pointed to a different spot on the map: Dallas.

"Look at the banks here," she suggested. "Just test the waters."

He submitted a few test applications. The phone started ringing within forty-eight hours. The demand was aggressive. He had to pump the brakes - he couldn't accept a job in a city a thousand miles away that he hadn't even moved to yet.

But the data was clear: Orlando was a safe haven, but Dallas was a boomtown.

Santos looked at the expiration date on his Indian Point orders. He looked at the emptiness of New York.

The "Charity Kid" would have stayed in the safety of his mother's house. The "Warrior" would have reenlisted for another war.

But the Survivor decided to try something new. He decided to go to Texas.

CHAPTER 15
THE TEXAS COLD WAR

January 2006 Dallas, Texas

Santos loaded the car in the dead of winter and made the twenty-hour drive south. It was a decompression chamber on wheels, the grey skyline of the Northeast fading into the flat, expansive horizon of Texas.

He pulled into a furnished apartment near DFW Airport, unpacked his bags, and started the new life. Taking a chance that the jobs would come as quickly as they did during the test run, he hit the pavement.

The offer came near the end of the second month. It was an Assistant Manager position at a growing bank about an hour's commute away.

He had to admit, a bit of Vanessa's materialism had rubbed off on him. He didn't just want a paycheck anymore; he wanted status. The title "Assistant Manager" felt good. The promise of rapid advancement felt better. And they didn't lie - the bank was growing fast, serving a specific clientele of lower-income workers.

Within six months, he was well on his way to his first promotion. It was perfect on paper.

But as he settled into the role, he began to see the machinery behind the curtain. The morals of the company didn't match the glossy brochures.

While the bank portrayed itself as a champion for the working class, behind the scenes, it was a predator. Santos watched the posting system with a sick feeling in his stomach. The algorithm was rigged to process debits before credits. A customer could have their paycheck deposited on the same day, but the system would drain their account with pending charges first, triggering a cascade of overdraft fees before the deposit hit.

It wasn't illegal - this was the Wild West before Dodd-Frank - but it was immoral. Why market to those who have the least, only to engineer a system that hits them with a mountain of fees?

He swallowed it for a while. "Buyer beware," he told himself. "Read the fine print."

He uncomfortably lived with the fact that there were no limits on how many fees the bank could charge in a day.

But the straw that broke the camel's back wasn't the fees. It was the ownership.

He discovered that the family who owned the bank also owned the collection agency where the charged-off accounts were sold.

The realization hit him like a splash of cold water. The system was rigged from top to bottom. They bled the customer dry with fees until the account collapsed, and then they sold the corpse to themselves to harvest the bones.

They made money on the failure of the very people they claimed to serve.

When his one-year anniversary arrived, they offered him a promotion to a new location opening up. It was half the distance from his home. It was the rapid advancement they had promised.

He turned it down.

He stopped playing the game. When people came in to inquire about opening accounts, he actively discouraged them. He warned them about the fee structures. His manager and the team were furious, but the District Manager - a man who seemed to understand the game better than anyone - gave him a surprising amount of grace.

He owed his success to the company, but he seemed to admire the conviction Santos had to walk away from it.

He found a job opening for a Relationship Manager position at a different bank, just ten minutes from his house. He didn't hesitate.

Within the month, he had interviewed with HR, the Branch Manager, and the District Manager. The minute he signed the job offer, he walked into his manager's office and handed in his two weeks' notice.

He had proved he could survive in the civilian world, but he had also proved something more important: He wouldn't sell his soul to do it.

2007–2009 THE GOOD YEARS & THE ETHOS

The next two years were a blur of construction. Not of a physical structure, but of a life he thought he was supposed to want.

At the new bank, he thrived. It was honest work, and for the first time, he had the freedom to do it his way.

Within the first year, he went from a Relationship Manager 1 to a Senior Relationship Manager.

He did it by throwing out the script. While other bankers were parroting company talking points and pushing the "Product of the Month," he remembered the lessons from the predatory bank.

He realized it was his duty to actually learn the ins and outs of the company he worked for. He learned every sector - annuities, Life Insurance Retirement Plans (LIRPs), investment sales.

He didn't have to push a product because he had the entire menu at his fingertips. He started by figuring out the customer's needs, and to his surprise, he found that unlike his previous employer, this bank actually had products that weren't designed to fail the customer.

By the end of his second year, he was fully licensed and making more on commission than his base pay. While other bankers were grinding out cold calls, his phone was ringing with referrals.

He was working in the Mid-Cities, the sleepy bedroom communities between Dallas and Fort Worth. Just to the north were three of the highest-earning cities in Texas. Every banker wanted those clients, but most were intimidated by them.

They saw a customer with two million dollars and froze.

Santos didn't. Some of those customers acted like they owned the world, but in his eyes, they wiped their ass with the same paper he did. Why would they intimidate him?

In time, even the ones who loved the line "Do you know who you're dealing with?" ended up in his chair, asking him to fund their next three-million-dollar home or find the right retirement fund so they could maintain their lifestyle after being forced out by their own boards.

These two years cemented his ethos. He was not willing to sacrifice his moral compass. He would not be just another car salesman, and he would not allow his drive for commission to be the reason someone else got screwed.

For Santos, the bottom line was never just about the balance sheet; it was about the weight of his word.

He viewed wealth not as a scorecard for dominance, but as a byproduct of doing things the right way. He chased growth relentlessly, yet never at the expense of his integrity or the people standing beside him.

To him, true power wasn't a resource to be hoarded or a lever of control - it was a tool to be shared. He wasn't interested in sitting on a throne above subordinates; he was dedicated to laying a foundation strong enough to lift everyone up.

He bought a house - a symbol of stability that the "Charity Kid" had never dreamed of owning.

He was engaged to Vanessa, the girl he had met during the transition. The wedding was set. The future was mapped.

But the map was wrong.

The deviation began with a career pivot that looked responsible on the surface but was purely tactical underneath.

Vanessa had been working in a call center, a grinding, metric-driven environment that she despised. She felt the headset and the scripts were beneath her; she was a main character forced to read the lines of an extra.

She didn't leave the call center because she discovered a passion for education or a desire to shape young minds. She left because teaching offered a "respectable" cover story and a schedule that aligned with her real ambition.

To her, the classroom wasn't a calling; it was a waiting room.

It was a strategic holding pattern that provided weekends and summers off - time she intended to use to chase the "dream job" in the Public Relations/Media industry that she was convinced was just around the corner. She wasn't building a career; she was killing time until the world finally recognized her status.

The rot started in the finances. Vanessa was chasing a career as a teacher, but her lifestyle was chasing the

Kardashians. She was materialistic, a collector of designer labels and expensive habits.

When Santos tried to apply the "Structure" of his new life to their bank accounts, the reaction was volatile. Discussions about budgets turned into arguments about control.

"You're suffocating me," she would say. "You're too controlling."

It was a gaslighting tactic, turning his desire for stability into a character flaw.

By early 2009, the emotional distance became physical. Vanessa started going out more. "Girls' nights" became frequent.

Then, she stopped answering her phone.

"My battery died," she would say the next morning, her eyes devoid of guilt. "We stayed with a friend."

The intuition that had kept Santos alive on Highway 1 started pinging. *Ambush imminent.*

It happened in May 2009, two weeks before the wedding.

Vanessa had dumped her purse out on the bed to switch bags. Among the lipstick and the keys, a slip of paper fluttered to the floor. Santos picked it up.

It was a hotel receipt. For a room in town. For a night she said she was staying with a girlfriend.

He confronted her. The lie was clumsy - "We split a room because we were tired" - but the truth was in her eyes.

She was having an affair.

Santos didn't scream. He didn't throw things. He activated the protocol he had used in the desert: *Assess. Decide. Execute.*

"This isn't the behavior of someone about to get married," he told her calmly. "Tell me the truth, or it's over."

She denied it. She doubled down.

"Then it's over," he said.

He grabbed his pillow and a blanket and walked downstairs to the living room. He called the wedding off.

If this were a movie, he would have packed his bags and driven into the sunset. But this was 2009. The housing market had collapsed. The economy was in freefall. They couldn't sell the house.

They were underwater.

So began The Cold War.

For the next eighteen months - from July 2009 to January 2011 - the house became a prison divided by a flight of stairs. Vanessa took the upstairs. Santos took downstairs.

It was a siege. They lived like ghosts, avoiding each other in the kitchen, passing in the hallway without speaking.

But while Santos was trying to maintain a respectful distance, Vanessa was waging a guerrilla war.

She weaponized the digital space. She gained access to his email accounts. Pretending to be Santos, she sent messages to his family back in New York. They were vicious, cruel emails, blaming his mother and his cousins for the breakup, insulting them, burning bridges with napalm.

Santos didn't know why his calls to New York were going unanswered. He didn't know why his family had suddenly turned cold, telling him, "We knew it wouldn't work out," before hanging up.

She had successfully cut his supply lines. He was isolated in enemy territory, surrounded by her friends in Texas who had already taken her side.

The only ally he had left was, ironically, Vanessa's best friend. She saw through the lies. She saw the quiet dignity Santos maintained in the basement while Vanessa spun chaotic webs upstairs.

But one ally wasn't enough to stop the bleeding.

By late 2010, the financial ruin was complete. Vanessa filed for bankruptcy to clear her own name, but she deftly maneuvered the joint debts - the credit cards she had maxed out, the loans she had taken - onto Santos.

She listed him as a creditor. She washed her hands, and he was left holding the bill.

A new year provided a new opportunity. Santos found an apartment. He prepared to extract.

He had very little left to take. The furniture, the appliances, the life they had built - she kept it all.

He packed his car. An air mattress. A TV. A bookshelf with some DVDs. His clothes.

He went to the garage to get the one thing that mattered: The Army Trunk.

It was a heavy, footlocker-style trunk. Inside was the history of his service. His Class A uniforms with the "Blood Rifles" pinned to the chest. The medals he had earned in the desert. The challenge coins given to him by commanders. The photos of the platoon outside the bunker. The photos of Akin.

It was gone.

He searched the garage. He searched the attic. He confronted her.

"I threw it out," she said, her voice flat. "It was taking up space."

She hadn't just thrown away a box. She had erased his history. She knew that the only thing he valued more than his financial stability was his Earned Self-Worth as a soldier. So she destroyed the proof.

Santos stood in the empty garage. He felt a rage so hot it was almost blinding, but underneath it, he felt a strange, cold clarity.

He realized then that he had been fighting the wrong enemy. He had been trying to be a "Good Man" to a woman who wanted to destroy him.

He turned around. He didn't yell. He didn't fight for the trash. He got into his car, the air mattress squeaking in the back seat.

He drove away. He was thirty years old. He had no money. He had no family speaking to him. He had no history. He was starting from scratch, stripped down to the studs.

But as he pulled onto the highway, putting distance between himself and the house, he realized one thing:

He was free.

CHAPTER 16

GROUND ZERO

January 2011 – 2012 Fort Worth, Texas

The Warrior lay on the ground.

The shrapnel of the last two years had torn him open. The betrayal, the isolation, the erasure of his history - it was a sucking chest wound. The "Charity Kid" was dead, buried under the weight of the debt and the shame. The "Soldier" was bleeding out.

The silence of the empty garage pressed down on him. The question hung in the air, heavy and suffocating: Is the wound fatal?

Santos looked at the empty space where his trunk used to be. He felt the phantom pain of his lost history. He felt the crushing weight of the bankruptcy she had forced onto him.

NO.

The word wasn't a thought; it was a command.

He reached into the darkness of his own mind and grabbed the tourniquet. He wrapped it around the hemorrhage of his emotions. He twisted the windlass. Twist. Twist. Lock.

The pain was blinding, but the bleeding stopped.

He let out a scream. It didn't make a sound in the quiet garage, but it roared in his skull. It wasn't a scream of pain. It was a scream of defiance.

I WILL NOT SURRENDER.

He stared at his reflection in the car window. He had no family in his corner. He had no partner. He had no past.

"I am NOT alone," he whispered.

As he stared into the dark glass, the reflection shifted. The tired, thirty-year-old man in the driveway faded, and The Warrior looked back. He was dusty, wearing the desert fatigues of 2004, but the expression on his face stopped Santos cold.

It wasn't the crooked, cynical grin of "validated disappointment" he had worn at the LaGuardia escalator. It was a genuine smile. A smile of empathy. Of understanding. Of true love.

And he wasn't alone.

Standing next to him, barely tall enough to reach the Warrior's hip, stood The Charity Kid. The boy with the "Can of Worms" bruise and the wide, watchful eyes looked up. He wasn't scared anymore. He was smiling that same smile.

They radiated something Santos had never felt before - a warmth that cut through the January cold. They radiated self-love.

Hand in hand, the Warrior and the Charity Kid stood in the glass, watching over the man they had become. They sparked a small fire in Santos's chest, illuminating a truth he had spent a lifetime running from:

Alone doesn't equal bad.

With the Warrior and the Charity Kid by his side, day one of who Santos truly was started to emerge. And with the glimmer of that small fire burning in his chest, Santos knew one thing for certain.

For the first time in his life, he was enough.

The reconstruction began on New Year's Day, 2011.

It was supposed to be a clean break. Santos had packed his car - the air mattress, the TV, the clothes. He had found a studio apartment, a small, solitary box where he could lick his wounds.

He had an appointment to sign the lease at 10:00 AM. The military taught him that if you are on time, you are late. So, he turned into the parking lot at 0950, ten minutes before his appointment.

It took Santos seconds to assess the scene. The leasing office was dark. There were no cars in the lot. There was a sign on the door.

His muscles tensed, his face flushing hot and red against the chill of the morning. The office was closed.

The panic tried to rise - a cold, familiar wave from the days of the shelter system - but he didn't let the fear take over. Not anymore. Santos no longer reacted in fear.

Improvise, Adapt, Overcome.

He reached for the door, a cool mist hitting his face, grounding him. He was already creating the plan. It hasn't escaped his subconscious yet, but all his training ensured that while the physical problem presented itself, the subconscious was working overtime to analyze and construct a logical, strategic course of action.

He pulled. Clank.

The sound of the locked door finalized it. He glanced at the sign: NEW YEARS DAY - CLOSED.

The disappointment was a physical blow. During his search, Santos had found this place - Location 1. It was an older studio, but it had the one thing he felt he needed to survive.

Just outside the sliding doors that led to the patio, around a small partition, was a little creek. The water flowed slowly, framed by two massive oak trees that sat on either side of the concrete slab.

The minute he saw it, he saw the hammock. He saw himself laying in it, watching the water, finding peace. He was so sure of it that he never even went to the second location on his list.

This was supposed to be the place.

But the door was locked. The hammock was gone.

Plan B burst out of his subconscious. Without a conscious thought, his muscles began to work. He didn't have a written list - consciously, he hadn't thought he needed contingencies. But his subconscious was a doomsayer.

At some point, he had saved the contact information for a second complex. He had allowed it to fade into obscurity, but his survival instinct had kept it in his back pocket.

As the mist continued to leave a layer of moisture on his face, Santos was already dialing. He had made the decision. If they picked up, the deal was set. He wasn't going to negotiate, and he wasn't going to beg. He wasn't in the game to mask his desperation with charm.

"Leasing office," a voice answered.

"Hi," Santos said, his voice flat and direct. "I'm in a bit of a jam. I need an apartment today."

He briefly explained the situation - homeless as of right now, cash in hand, ready to move. The most he hoped for was to be added to a waitlist or pushed up a few spots.

"Well, you are in luck," the leasing agent said. "Unfortunately, we do not have one ready today, but there is one that is getting painted right now. It will be ready tomorrow."

"Really?" Santos exclaimed, the tension in his shoulders dropping an inch. "Okay. When can I see it?"

"Come on by anytime today. I can't show you that specific unit because of the fumes, but I have one exactly like it that has someone moving in tomorrow as well."

This was the best he could hope for. He wasn't going to let delay or indecision lose him this chance.

"Okay. I will be over in about ten minutes. Do you mind drawing up all the papers so if everything is good, we can sign today?"

"We'll have them ready."

He hung up. The crisis was managed. The objective was secured.

But as he walked back to his car, the reality of the timeline settled in. He had to survive one more night.

It required one final act of humility. He had to drive back to the house - the house he owned, the house where his ex was living - and ask for a twenty-four-hour extension.

He walked in, bowl in hand, and slept one last night in the basement of his own life. He lay on the sofa like a guest with a mortgage, an inconvenience to the person who got to keep the home that his Veteran's Home Loan benefits had paid for.

The next day, he moved into the new apartment. It didn't have the creek, and it didn't have the oak trees. But when he walked in, it smelled of fresh paint and possibility.

The next two years were a montage of discipline. Santos treated his recovery like a deployment.

0500 Hours: Gym. Two hours a day. He tore his muscles down and built them back up, replacing the stress-weight of the "Cold War" with armor. He lifted until his arms shook, pushing the physical pain to drown out the emotional noise.

0900 Hours: Work. He attacked the debt she had left him with a vengeance. Every paycheck was a strategic strike. He lived on nothing, throwing every spare dollar at the creditors.

Slowly, the balance sheets turned from red to black.

He furnished the apartment. Not with air mattresses, but with real furniture. A couch. A table. A bed frame.

He built a sanctuary.

But a sanctuary can be a lonely place.

By late 2011, the "Warrior" was strong, but he was isolated. He was tired of the bar scene, tired of the alcohol, tired of the noise. He wanted connection, but he didn't know where to find it.

"Why don't you go to church?" a friend from New York joked on the phone.

Santos laughed. He wasn't looking for God. He was looking for something to do on a Sunday morning that didn't involve a hangover.

But there was a small church nearby - a tiny storefront operation in a shopping strip near his apartment complex. It was unassuming. It didn't look like an institution; it looked like a living room.

He went.

He didn't find fire and brimstone. He found the Pastor's sons. They were younger, full of energy. One was a carefree spirit, a mess of charisma. The other was a thinker - a presumptuous, philosophical mind who loved to debate the nature of existence.

They became the outlet Santos had been starving for. Over the years, Santos had tried to pursue his BA, but he found even Online University insufferable. It wasn't the difficulty; it was the rigidity. The idea of focusing on one or two subjects at a time felt like running in mud.

But the real enemy were the essays. The professors didn't want originality; they wanted conformity. The grading rubrics proved it. You were not allowed to pick the subject. You were given two or three pre-determined topics, and if you didn't follow the flow, you lost critical points.

University wasn't a place for original ideas; it was a place where the so-called subject matter experts confirmed that you followed the prescribed narrative.

But here, with these brothers, the rubric was thrown out the window. Santos met people who openly played - or allowed him to play - the "Devil's Advocate" until the objections reached their absurd conclusions.

He was naturally drawn to that circle.

We talked about how the universe was created. We discussed String Theory and Quantum Theory. We debated Intelligent Design versus Creationism versus Evolutionary Theory. These were the topics Santos found in these people.

We had beliefs, but it was okay to question those beliefs - and not only question them, but question them until you were able to get to a logical conclusion.

There was no animosity. No personal feelings were hurt. This was academic; this was solving the equation. And when there wasn't a conclusion to be had, it wasn't "feelings" that guided the final proposition - it was reason and logic. If one set of propositions weighed more logically than the other, then that, at least for the time being, was the best solution.

Santos found himself putting the expansion of his knowledge on overdrive. It bled into his professional life - he learned new market strategies, figuring out how to best leverage a client's equity to borrow from their own assets, ensuring they were less reliant on financial firms.

He was building financial freedom for others while seeking spiritual freedom for himself.

He consumed information voraciously. He picked up books from Richard Dawkins and William Lane Craig. He read Stephen Hawking's The Grand Design and God, Stephen Hawking and the Multiverse. He read the Bible and heavy theology books. He read The Matrix and Philosophy. He read short stories from C.S. Lewis.

Even his entertainment shifted. His favorite genre, Supernatural Horror, became a dramatic window into the world beyond the veil.

The existential questions were never answered, but they were satiated. Santos found himself in this time; he found some peace.

It wasn't one specific point or argument that finally broke the dam, but a specific message.

One Sunday, the Pastor spoke about David and Moses. He mentioned Abraham, Peter, and Paul. All men who, by all standards, were broken or long fallen. But God chose them to be His messengers.

He chose the weak. He chose the broken. He chose the man who persecuted and murdered believers to be the shining light on the hill.

The Pastor's voice cut through the room: "God used those of us who have been through hell and back to prove to the world that if this man, if this person is able to change, if this person is able to receive the forgiveness and grace of God... then anyone can receive it."

He read from 2 Corinthians 12: "And he said unto me, My grace is sufficient for thee: for my strength is made perfect in weakness. Most gladly therefore will I rather glory in my infirmities, that the power of Christ may rest upon me."

It was that evening.

Santos sat on his rolling chair in the living room, the apartment quiet. His computer was pulled up to YouTube, and in the search bar, he had typed: "Prayer to be saved."

As the video played, he closed his eyes and prayed.

An unnatural amount of tears began flowing down his face. It was like a fire hydrant of his past had been sheared off - a waterfall of all the rot and bile that had festered for thirty years pouring out of his eyes.

Drowning in those tears, words couldn't leave his body, yet he audibly heard himself praying. His hands were shaking, his breath coming in jagged inhalations and forced exhalations.

Then, silence.

"Amen."

His eyes opened slowly, but he was no longer in his chair. He was on his knees on the floor. His face was soaked with tears, his mouth dry as a desert. He looked up. His computer screen was black. Not just the screensaver - it had gone into sleep mode from long inactivity.

How long have I been here? How long was I kneeling?

The questions sat in the air, with no answer in sight. He got up, knowing that this wasn't a debate. The question didn't need answering.

His first act of faith was simply to rise from his knees, not look at the clock, rinse off his face, and go lay in bed for the night.

With one final statement, the world went black.

"Thank you, Lord."

In that moment of peace, Santos felt the tectonic plates of his soul finally settle. The spiritual void - the one he had tried to fill with alcohol, with work, with anger - was closed. It was a restoration that only a Divine intervention could have orchestrated.

With that internal foundation finally solid, he realized there was now safe ground to build something else. The space was prepared for the only thing still missing: the commitment of a lifelong helpmate.

He didn't go back to the bars. The party scene was for the twenty-year-old crowd, a chaotic noise he had outgrown. Instead, Santos turned to the only tool he knew how to wield with precision: the internet.

He signed up for dating apps and plunged into the deep end. He wasn't looking for a savior anymore. He was just looking for someone who was real.

CHAPTER 17
THE IRON LINE

February 2013 Fort Worth, Texas

By 2013, Santos had categorized the dating world into a binary code: Predators and Prey. Or maybe it was Liars and Fools.

Of course, these categories fit both sexes, but from a male perspective, the landscape looked specific. Women often played the role of the damsel in distress or the princess waiting for Prince Charming. To Santos, this was a performance. You hook the guy with sweetness, secure the ring, and then the battle for control begins. He had watched friends get married, and within months, their wives transformed from free spirits into nagging stereotypes.

But the men were just as guilty. They played their own pathetic role: the lazy husband who wants to drink beer in the garage, eat wings, and play *Call of Duty* for nine hours straight, only to crawl into bed and poke his wife expecting intimacy like he was turning a key in an ignition. It was as if everyone had access to centuries of data on what didn't work in relationships, yet they willingly submitted to the stereotype.

Santos found it revolting. He didn't want someone who "played the game."

He was tired. The "Warrior Reconstruction" had worked - he was fit, he was solvent, and he was stable - but he was also cynical. The dating apps were a parade of unoriginality. Every profile claimed, "I'm not like other girls," and every date ended with the same feigned innocence followed by the same predictable slide into casual intimacy.

He had cracked the code, and he hated it. He stopped trying.

He started sending copy-paste messages - generic, low-effort bait to see who would bite. It was a game to pass the time, a way to be lonely with an audience.

Then came the notification.

Message from [May]: "Did you really send me a copy/paste message?"

Santos stared at the phone. His first instinct was defense - *What's my cover story?*

But then he looked at the words again. She wasn't playing the game. She was auditing it.

He decided to drop the shield.

"Yup," he typed back. "Kinda tired of the dating scene so I put little effort into it."

He expected silence. Instead, he got a conversation.

They exchanged numbers. They met. And for the first time in years, Santos found himself sitting across from someone who didn't feel like a "Non-Player Character."

May was a walking smile, a radiator of warmth that thawed the edges of his cynicism. She was the "Comfort Blanket" he hadn't realized he needed. She was vibrant, honest, and painfully real. She didn't have the calculated defenses that Santos had spent a decade perfecting.

The year 2013 seemed to fly by. Santos and May found genuine peace in each other.

May's family met Santos and, defying his expectations, accepted him into the circle. This wasn't the hostile "meet the parents" trope. He clicked with May's dad and uncles - hard-working blue-collar guys.

Her dad was a jack-of-all-trades and a master of none. He was the guy you called to MacGyver a starter onto a car, but he was also the guy who might install a light fixture that, with the flip of a switch, blew out the entire breaker panel.

Santos would laugh about it, but internally, frustration would sometimes bubble up. *Confidence should be reserved for what you know, not what you think you know,* he would think.

But he stowed the frustration away because, deep down, he knew the truth: May's dad was the father he never had.

And May was the comfort he never had. She cheered him on. She supported him. She made him feel like a human being, not just a man-shaped form drifting through the world.

But the "Warrior" wasn't ready to retire.

Deep down, Santos still believed that his only true value lay in his ability to fight. The domestic quiet terrified him. The silence of a Sunday afternoon felt like an ambush waiting to happen.

He missed the tribe. He missed the simplicity of orders. He missed the *thump-thump* of the .50 cal, which made more sense to him than the quiet terror of intimacy.

He had been talking to a recruiter for the Texas National Guard. He decided to test her. It was a subconscious sabotage - a way to see if she would run before he got too attached.

"I'm thinking about reenlisting," he told her over dinner. "Going back in."

He watched her face, waiting for the "I'll support you" speech or the "Please don't go" drama.

He got neither.

"I don't think I could be in a military relationship," she said.

Her voice was calm, but the boundary was ironclad. She wasn't issuing an ultimatum; she was stating a fact about her own capacity. She knew who she was, and she knew she couldn't marry a war.

She drew a line in the sand. *Ball's in your court, Santos.*

He looked at the line. On one side was the Safe Choice: Reenlist. Go back to the desert. Embrace the "Alone Mentality" in a crowd of soldiers. It was dangerous, yes, but he knew how to survive it. He knew the Rules of Engagement.

On the other side was the Hard Choice: Stay. Take the hand of this woman. Trust her. Risk being broken again without a flak jacket to protect his heart.

He looked at her. He saw the empathy in her eyes - not the pity of the "Charity Kid" days, but genuine care.

He dusted over the line.

"Okay," he said. "No military."

He chose the girl. He chose the future. He thought he was choosing peace.

December 2013 arrived - a cold night in Rockefeller Center. Santos had already asked her dad for permission. He had asked her "Pepa," who was battling cancer, for permission.

With the green light from both, he held May in his arms as they peered up at the bright lights of the tree, shining as bright as the future that lay ahead of them.

"May, I have never felt for anyone the way I feel for you. You have made me feel like I never thought I could feel. So I wanted to ask, would you give me the greatest gift that anyone could give? Would you take my hand and be my wife?"

Silence. It felt like an eternity, but it was only two seconds.

She turned. "Yes. Of course."

But looking into his eyes with that mischievous smile she often wore, she added, "You didn't get down on one knee."

Santos stood there, smiling. "It's too crowded."

And it was. The mood and moment were right, but deep down, a small voice from the basement of his psyche whispered: *Of course you didn't kneel. You don't kneel to anyone. That version of you is gone.*

2014 – 2019 THE CONSTRUCTION

If the choice to stay was the foundation, the next five years were the framing, the drywall, and the roof. They set out to build the monument that every generation is told to worship: The American Dream.

The wedding was set for November 2014. What should have been a major gathering turned into a small, somber celebration. Just over a month prior, May's beloved grandfather - the patriarch of the family - had lost his battle with cancer.

The family was exhausted, emotionally drained. For some, it was too soon to celebrate; for others, the thought of travel was like picking at a scab. Santos and May understood. They encouraged people to stay home if they needed to. They didn't need the sight of a big wedding to prop our egos up.

They said the vows, they danced, and that evening was the beginning of their life.

He attacked this new mission with the same ferocity he had applied to clearing rooms in Samarra. The objective was clear: Normalcy. Stability. Success.

Then, 2016 brought them something he never in his wildest dreams thought he wanted, nor knew he needed.

Santos and May welcomed their baby boy, naming him in honor of the grandfather they had just mourned.

He introduced him to the world, and in those first few moments that he held him, an IED went off in his heart. Every single damn wall he had built to protect himself shattered into splinters.

This squiggling little bundle, who couldn't even control his own limbs, did something not one other person in this universe was able to do. Not even May. He brought Santos to his knees. Yes, he had knelt before God for salvation, because God was love, God was pure. People, on the other hand, did not deserve his reverence.

But this little boy? He was everything.

Without thinking, he made a decision at that moment. This boy would have everything he didn't. He would feel loved and protected. He would be sheltered from the world's horrors and treated with respect.

He knew that as the boy grew, he would have to be the tough guy, because the world would eventually set out to destroy his innocence. But at least for the first few years, this little child would be treated to the life Santos could only wish for in his own childhood.

After renting a townhome, then a small house, in 2017 they bought the house in an upper-middle-class town north of Dallas. It wasn't just a structure; it was a fortress. It had the manicured lawn, the open floor plan, and the patio where one is supposed to sit and drink lemonade while watching the sunset.

It was the physical manifestation of "Making It."

He climbed the corporate ladder. He traded the desert fatigues for a suit and tie, refining the persona of the "Good Man." He learned the corporate dialect - synergy, deliverables, quarterly projections. He became "The Provider."

The "Warrior" was escorted to the basement of his psyche, locked behind a heavy steel door, and told to stay quiet.

We don't need you anymore, he told him. *The war is over. We are civilians now.*

And for a while, the illusion held. He fully embraced the role. He was "Dad." He even had the "Best Dad Ever" t-shirt to prove it.

He looked at his life and saw a checklist with every box ticked. Career? Check. House? Check. Wife? Check. Kid? Check.

He told himself, *This is it. We won.*

He bought into the narrative that if you just work hard enough, if you just build the walls high enough, you reach a state of perpetual happiness. He thought he was living in the movie ending - the part where the credits roll over a scene of a happy couple laughing on a porch.

But he forgot the lesson he had taught Vanessa years ago: "The dream job doesn't exist; that's why it is a dream."

Now, he was living a new variation of that lie. He was telling himself, "The American Dream exists."

He didn't realize that the scene on the porch is a snapshot, not a documentary. You don't get to just sit and drink the lemonade. Someone has to squeeze the lemons. Someone has to wash the pitcher. Someone has to pay the mortgage on the porch. Someone has to worry about the weeds growing in the cracks of the patio.

He was working himself to the bone to maintain the set design of a play that he didn't realize was a tragedy.

He thought he had buried the trauma under the foundation of the house. He thought the "Warrior" was dormant. He thought the "Charity Kid" was satisfied with the toys and the gadgets he could now afford to buy.

He didn't know yet that peace was just a different kind of war.

And the enemy was already inside the wire.

CHAPTER 18

THE LOOPHOLE

2020 – April 2022 North Texas / The Border

Santos was antsy. He was itching to get back in the fight.

He felt age coming on, seeing the "Warrior" slipping away in the mirror. At one point, the Facebook groups for 11B Infantrymen were filled with guys just like him - hard-charging veterans of the surge. But now? He was the BDU-wearing Boomer. The groups were filled with eighteen-year-olds who weren't even born when the Towers fell.

He saw his youth slipping away. It wasn't that he wasn't fulfilled by his family life, but this was a man who had been "in the fight" for thirty years. Now, he was expected to sit out to pasture.

When the Texas Defense Force set up a recruiting table at the VA, Santos was like a fly to a flame.

This was the answer. It felt like a loophole in the universe. Minimal danger. Short deployments. Focused on storm recovery and border support. This time, Santos told himself he wasn't lying to keep the peace. The truth was the compromise.

May must have seen it in his eyes. Looking back, Santos knew she agreed reluctantly. She threw him a bone, thinking this seemed fairly harmless. Let him have his midlife crisis, she probably thought.

But as with anything related to the military - whether state or federal - the machine has a way of making a man choose between his family and the uniform.

For Santos, the choice was never about abandoning his family. It was about protecting the sanctuary he had built for them.

He would sit on his back porch, looking at the manicured lawn and the safe street, and he would feel a crushing weight of debt. He was a homeless kid from the Bronx who had been allowed to grasp a slice of the American Dream. He had made it. But he knew that this dream was fragile.

He looked at the news, and he didn't see politics; he saw poison. The reports of trafficking - drugs and humans - weren't just headlines to him. They were threats at the gate.

He looked at his five-year-old son playing in the safety of their home, and a dark vision would override the peace. He imagined his boy on a playground, foaming at the mouth because he found a small, colorful baggy that looked like candy.

Instead of gumdrops, it was fentanyl.

It wasn't a hypothetical. It had happened to a little girl not far from where they lived. It was happening all around them. Law Enforcement Officers were carrying Narcan just to survive a traffic stop. Thirty miles south, in Dallas, junkies filled the emergency rooms. Half of them were overdosing not because they took something, but because they merely touched a needle or a baggy from another user.

Santos felt a visceral rage at the blindness of the suburbs. People were sleeping while the wolves were chewing through the fence.

He thought about the victims. These were men and women who had lives ahead of them. Some might have continued the cycle of generational poverty, but some would have bucked the trend - just like Santos did. They could have made something of themselves, had it not been for that one night they tore a ligament or sprained an ankle.

The doctor prescribed an opioid. Two pills too many, and the brain flicked a switch. Addiction hit. Then came the second prescription, then the third with a warning. Then came the referral to pain management, then the prognosis that the pain should be gone.

But the pain was real - it was the brain projecting signals to be fed that beautiful, numbing medication.

When you live in the ghetto, a doctor refusing a script isn't an issue. It's just a matter of a phone call.

And as the ER nurse pumps the chest for the last time and the Narcan packets fall to the floor, that person who would have been the first in her family to graduate college lies limp. Eyes staring at nothing. Chest bare. Instead of the acrylic nails she once got every week, her hands are covered in dirt and dried fluids from the John she serviced to get the twenty dollars for the hit she needed.

This was what Santos saw. He saw himself in that woman. He saw himself in every dead junkie that laid in the baking sun until the smell became too intense and someone decided the body needed to be "handled."

He saw himself in them because it could have easily been him.

Santos once had a large family - aunts, uncles, cousins from Massachusetts to Miami, North Carolina to California. But every year, the word came: this one died, or that one passed. It was so common that Santos barely paid attention anymore. The only ones left were names that were supposed to mean something to him, but he had no clue who they were. They had ended up in jail or dead in the streets.

It would have taken only a left turn when he turned right for his life to be completely different.

This was his time to stand up once more.

I'll be damned if I stand idly by, he told himself. I won't allow my son to grow up in a world where we allow drug smugglers to run supply routes without consequence.

He wasn't going to sit there while the government, which was supposed to protect its citizens from the poisons of the world, made it easier for snake oil salesmen to push their bottles of toxin on their kids.

The day finally came. His trunk was packed. The ruck and two duffels were ready.

"Three months," he told May. "Three months and I'll be back home, and everything will be fine."

But he felt it deep inside, a vibration in his gut that he ignored. This will not end well. This is a bad idea.

He pushed the thought down. For the first time in his life, he felt secure. He had a strong woman by his side. A son who was an absolute blessing - smart, energetic, loving. May was the picture of strength and stability.

In his civilian life, he left before anyone was awake and got home as his son was going to sleep. Sure, he did the honey-do list on weekends. But he convinced himself this deployment was just a blip.

Three months. That's all.

But three months turned into six.

Somewhere in that time, Santos and May drifted. Santos, who used to be perceptive, didn't see that May was struggling even before he left. He didn't hear the silence behind the words "We got this" or "Don't worry about us." He didn't see her eyes screaming Don't go or I need you here.

May thought if she stayed silent, she could hang on for three months. But when it turned to six, the foundation cracked.

Despite living his own childhood without a functional father, Santos allowed his son's intelligence to fool him. He convinced himself the boy was mature enough to handle it. But a mother's love cannot replace a father's foundation. What Santos had worked so hard to build started to crumble.

Santos managed the optics. On FaceTime, he was strategic. He only showed the good.

He never mentioned the times his location took fire. May doesn't need that stress, he told himself. She has enough on her plate.

He didn't tell her about the times he had to draw his weapon because someone was trying to breach the fence. Operational Security dictated silence, but so did fear - fear that May would tell the wrong person and cause a PR outcry because God forbid anyone in uniform defended themselves.

He didn't mention the nightly potshots from the cartels, just trying to antagonize the Americans who were forbidden by the Rules of Engagement to fire back across the border.

So, they lived two lives. The life they showed each other on camera - a lie wrapped in good intent that slowly poisoned their fairy tale. And the real life they lived apart, holding out for three months that dragged into six.

April 2022

Three weeks before Santos was coming home for good.

He had just gotten over Covid, which took him back almost twenty years to the day of his Basic Training pneumonia. This time, there was no room in the hospital, so he was quarantined in a hotel. The pneumonia only took twenty-five pounds this time instead of thirty. Thankfully, he didn't fall comatose, or he wouldn't have been discovered for days given the piss-poor logistics for sick soldiers.

He received approval for a four-day leave to finish his sick profile at home. He would return only to train his replacement for two weeks, and then, papers in hand, the mission was over.

It didn't take long after walking in the door.

May's smile was gone. The hug was cold. The look was defeat.

"Hey babe, everything ok?"

"Yeah, I am just tired."

Nothing more.

That was when the subconscious you should have known came rushing in like a tsunami, one wave after another.

Santos sat down, his uniform top unbuttoned, bootlaces untied. He sat on his sofa, and he drowned.

There was no noble welcome home. The minuscule hope he had nursed - that maybe he would turn the corner and see balloons and signs, that for once in his miserable life he would come home to pride and longing - that hope left his body. It escaped like the last bubbles of air from a drowning man.

May had left the house at some point, probably to go to work. But Santos was still sitting on that sofa.

Beer in hand. He looked down. Three on the floor. One in my hand. Okay, two more left. Gonna have to get a case soon.

He set the bottle down and eyed the coffee table.

There sat two medicine bottles he had taken out of his assault pack - a bag that was really just a glorified carry-on. Prescription blood pressure medication. Prescription sleeping medication.

Santos sat there, seeing his hands as if through a periscope.

Who opened the bottle and poured the pills into my hand? he thought.

The periscope shifted left. What does that say in the text message to May? What am I about to send her?

The periscope shifted right. Why do I have these two meds mixed in my hands? I'm in no shape to figure out which are which.

Damn. They are all in my hands. I need to do something before the dog gets a pill.

He shifted his gaze further right.

There was his nine-year-old dog. She was staring at him with those knowing eyes. She was one of those wise dogs you swear must have been a human in another life.

What are you looking at?

And as if she answered him, the voice cut through the fog.

What do you think will happen when your son walks in, with the excitement of the world, only to find you laying there? Woe is you! But what about him?

What? What are you talking about? Pills still firmly in his hand, his finger hovering over the send button.

What about May? Look at what six months did to her. What do you think will happen in a lifetime? You left her! You left her to fend for herself! She didn't ask for this.

She told you day one she couldn't be a military wife. She did right by you. She trusted you to honor her wishes. She was honest. And you spat in her face.

You abandoned her. You abandoned your son!

The dog's eyes didn't blink.

And now, when you have the opportunity to salvage the little you have left, you want to be no better than your own father? You want to damage your son beyond repair? You want to strip any possibility of restoring happiness and faith back in May's heart?

You broke the vows once, and you're about to do it again.

You! Disgust! Me!

And again, Santos found himself on his knees.

Guttural sobs escaped his throat. He was no longer drowning; he was gasping for air. Between the sobs and the gasps came a pleaful Why?

Why did I not listen to my gut? Why had I not seen the signs? Why did I have to feel that selfish need to retrieve a person I once was for a life I no longer live?

This time, the cries did not lead to confusion or despair. It wasn't going to lead to a neighborhood church and a studio apartment.

This time, Santos knew that the fight wasn't on any desert land or border crossing. The fight was right here, in his very living room.

He knew he still had to go back for the two weeks; there was no question about that. Legally, the state could bring charges against him if he didn't finish the mission. But he knew something else.

If he could keep his marriage treading water for that short time, he was going to dedicate everything he had going forward to making right what he had made wrong.

He dropped the pills. He closed the phone.

He stood up.

CHAPTER 19

THE BREAKER SWITCH

May 2022 – Mid 2023 North Texas

Santos came home from the border with a plan. He had looked into the abyss on that sofa, and he had pulled back.

He decided to treat his life like a broken piece of equipment. If he just applied the right maintenance, the right parts, and the right amount of elbow grease, he could fix it.

He put the mask on. He became the "Good Man" again.

For two years, he did everything right. He went to therapy. He communicated. He was present. He wore the "Best Dad Ever" shirt, and he made sure his actions matched the slogan. He did it so well that he actually started to believe it himself. The house was calm. The bank accounts were stable. The "Warrior" was quiet.

Things started looking good again.

But the universe has a way of testing the structural integrity of a mask.

In late 2022, May was pregnant. They were hopeful. But a little over a month later, she miscarried.

The way Santos took it was different than anything else he had experienced. He took it hard, feeling the crushing weight of the loss, but he also took it numbly. The "Good Man" couldn't crumble, so he processed the grief through a filter of duty.

They found out during DNA testing that he was a boy. They named him. Santos thought it would be nice to get a time capsule tube to put letters and a few little trinkets in. They intended to bury it, to give him a resting place.

Instead, they kept it in their living room. At first, they thought it was avoidance, but recently it had changed into a reminder to keep him in their hearts.

To the point that this past Christmas, they hung a stocking for him. "Santa" left two candies for their two living boys as a way for them to always remember their angel brother.

They mourned, but they kept moving.

A few months after the miscarriage, May was pregnant again. This time, she carried just short of full term. Pre-eclampsia caused an early delivery, but in 2023, they were blessed with their second son.

But blessings in their world rarely came without complications.

Their oldest son was navigating neurodivergence. May was battling major depression, which had evolved from severe postpartum depression. Santos's own struggles with PTSD and increasing anxiety were simmering under the surface.

And now, this new blessing arrived with his own battles - he struggled with swallowing and had a malformed ear. It was mainly cosmetic, but they made the hard choice to fix it so he wouldn't have to deal with the cruelty of the world later.

They were a house of two divergent sons and a marriage still trying to figure out where to put the rocks of their foundation back on.

Despite it all, they persevered. They found the mutual strength to do what was needed, even if it was just getting through one day and feeding the boys. They told themselves that they were in this together. They struggled, they yelled, they cried, but they believed that those within their four walls were all that mattered.

But a life built on suppressed trauma isn't a fortress; it's a house of cards. It stands tall and looks impressive, but it lacks a foundation.

It takes barely a sigh to knock it all down.

The sigh that came was a hurricane.

In early 2025, the phone rang. The man who had stolen his childhood - the man who had planted the seeds of rage and inadequacy deep in his gut - was dead.

His father was gone.

Santos expected relief. He expected the final closing of a chapter. He thought he would feel the weight lift off his shoulders.

Instead, the Breaker Switch tripped.

What he thought should have been closure only served to rip open every wound he had spent forty years packing down into the deep, dark recesses of his subconscious. The death of the monster didn't kill the monster; it released his ghost.

And then, his body joined the revolt.

For the better part of a year, he had been fighting with the VA, trying to explain that the machinery was breaking down. He wasn't just "sad." His biology was failing. But now, triggered by the psychological hurricane, the physical collapse accelerated.

It seemed like his body was now in a fight with itself.

The blood pressure would skyrocket to dangerous levels, so the doctors would add medication. Then his blood pressure would tank, and he would pass out in the kitchen. My heart raced without reason, a drum beating a retreat in his chest while he was sitting perfectly still.

The pain changed. It was no longer the dull ache of old rucksack injuries. It was like lava was flowing through his veins, seeping into the muscles, burning from the inside out.

Then his mind betrayed him.

He would be in the middle of a conversation, looking at May or his son, and the words would just... stop.

He knew what he wanted to say. He could see the sentence in his head. But the connection between the brain and the mouth was severed. He would stand there, stuttering, a terrifying silence filling the room as he realized he had absolutely no idea what was happening.

And then came the fatigue.

"Tired" is too small a word. "Exhaustion" doesn't cover it. It was a cellular shutdown.

It was as if the literal life energy was draining out of him, and at any moment, he would shut down into power save mode. Every day, he would have to take two to four hours in bed just to get through the daylight hours.

He wasn't sleeping; he was recharging a battery that could no longer hold a charge.

He looked at May. He looked at the distance between them.

There was no other man. There was no other woman. The "betrayal" wasn't a sordid affair in a motel room. It was something far more tragic.

It was the realization that the "Vows" hadn't been broken by sex; they had been broken by silence. They had been broken when he left for the border. They had been broken by the years he spent mentally deployed even when he was physically present.

She was standing right there, but she was miles away. And he didn't have the energy to swim across the ocean to get her.

So, he retreated.

He couldn't control his body. He couldn't control his blood pressure. He couldn't control the past.

But he could control the blocks.

He sat on the couch, the "Shell" taking over the controls. He turned on the Xbox. He loaded *Minecraft*.

In that world, if a monster came, he could build a wall. If he needed resources, he could mine them. If he died, he could respawn.

It was a digital bunker. A place where the rules were fair and the outcomes were predictable.

But as he sat there, hour after hour, building castles that didn't exist, something started to shift.

He had started Ketamine therapy - a last-ditch effort to reset the wiring in his brain. And in those sessions, detached from the pain of the body, he started to see the battlefield differently.

He had always looked at these obstacles - the abuse, the war, the betrayal, the illness - as enemies to be defeated. He thought he had to *fight* the depression. He thought he had to *fight* the fatigue.

But as he stared at the screen, placing one block after another, a quiet epiphany began to rise through the lava in his veins.

Maybe the "Breaker Switch" didn't trip to hurt him. Maybe it tripped to save him.

When a circuit is overloaded, the breaker trips to prevent the house from burning down. His system was overloaded. The pain, the fatigue, the brain fog - it was his body screaming, *STOP*.

Stop trying to be the hero. Stop trying to earn your worth. Stop running.

He realized that the obstacle wasn't in the way of the path. The obstacle *was* the path.

He wasn't being buried; he was being planted.

The darkness of the "Shell" wasn't a tomb. It was a cocoon. He was being forced to sit still, to be stripped of his physical strength, his sharp wit, and his "Provider" status, so that he could finally meet the man who lived underneath all of it.

He wasn't ready to come out yet. The "Shell" still needed to protect the soft, growing thing inside.

So he sat on the couch. He built his walls. He waited.

He didn't know it then, but the brown envelope was already in the mail. The final test was coming. But this time, he wouldn't fight it with fists or rifles.

He would fight it with the one thing they couldn't take from him.

His truth.

CHAPTER 20
THE PROXY WAR

Late 2025 - North Texas

The brown envelope from the VA sat on the side table for two weeks.

Santos didn't open it because he already knew what was inside. It was another "No." Another standardized form letter telling him that his reality didn't match their regulations.

He was in the middle of a ten-week short-term disability leave from work. He had to take it. He physically couldn't function. It wasn't just that he was tired; it was that his body had seemingly decided to go on strike. Neurologically, he was misfiring. Physically, he was drained.

He had stopped the spiral into the abyss, but he hadn't started the climb out. He was just... existing.

He looked at the envelope. Here we go again, he thought. Another round of begging a doctor to believe me.

He had spent months pleading with specialists. He asked the cardiologist why his heart raced. The doctor gave him a beta-blocker. He asked the neurologist why he couldn't find words. The doctor gave him a scan that came back "normal." He begged his primary care doctor to stop sending him to different silos and find someone who could look at the whole building.

That request was treated as unreasonable. That's not how medicine works, they implied. We treat the symptom, not the ghost.

But Santos knew there was a ghost.

Something triggered him that Tuesday. Maybe it was the dust settling on the unopened envelope. Maybe it was the sheer frustration of being a problem that no one wanted to solve.

If they won't look at the big picture, he decided, I will paint it for them.

He opened his laptop. He wasn't a doctor, but he was an Analyst. He knew how to find patterns in data. He knew how to track a discrepancy.

He went down the rabbit hole.

He didn't search for "anxiety" or "fatigue." He searched for the locations. Dujail. Balad. Taji. He searched for the dates. 2004. 2005.

And then, the algorithm fed him the missing piece.

Burn Pits.

He read the reports. He read the chemical compositions of the smoke that had hung over FOB Vanguard every single day. Plastics. Medical waste. Styrofoam. Diesel fuel. Rubber. Human waste.

He remembered the smell. It wasn't just a nuisance; it was a chemical weapon they had inflicted on themselves.

He read about the long-term effects: Neurological damage. Vascular inflammation. Autoimmune disorders. Chronic fatigue.

It was a checklist of his life.

He didn't stop there. He dug into the unit logs. He found the "Particulate Matter" reports from the DOD itself, documents that admitted the air quality in the Salah ad Din province during their deployment was "hazardous to human health."

He felt a cold, hard rage settling in his chest. It wasn't the hot, reactive anger of the "Warrior." It was the cold, calculating fury of the "Investor" who realizes he's been sold a fraudulent asset.

He wasn't crazy. He wasn't weak. He was poisoned.

He realized then that he wasn't fighting a medical condition; he was fighting a cover-up. The VA operated on a "deny until they die" strategy. They counted on the veteran giving up. They counted on the fatigue wearing them down.

They don't know who they're dealing with, he thought. They think they're dealing with a tired old man. They forgot they're dealing with a man who cleared rooms in the dark.

He called it "The Proxy War."

He wasn't fighting insurgents with rifles anymore. He was fighting bureaucrats with PDFs.

He spent the next three weeks building his case. He didn't just fill out the forms. He built a dossier. He printed out the EPA studies on burning plastic. He printed out the

DOD air quality reports. He highlighted the dates. He cross-referenced his medical records with the exposure symptoms.

He wrote a "Nexus Letter" - a document linking his service to his sickness - that was so detailed it could have been a court filing.

He treated his own body like a crime scene, and he was the lead detective.

As he worked, something shifted in the house. The "Shell" cracked open, not to reveal the "Warrior" or the "Charity Kid," but to reveal a synthesis of them all.

He looked at May. He saw the exhaustion in her eyes, the way she managed the boys, the house, and him.

He felt guilt. He looked at the laundry pile he couldn't lift. He looked at the lawn he couldn't mow.

May no longer gave him "the look" of frustration when he tapped out after one task. But he saw it in her eyes. It was hard on her. She was carrying the weight of the household, a weight he used to pride himself on bearing.

But he also saw that granite determination she used to have. She inspired him.

So, he pushed. Just a little.

It might be picking up the paper plates the boys left on the floor. It might be emptying the third dishwasher load of the day.

He tried to cook more. He used to be the chef of the house, but he had stopped so long ago he wondered if the muscle memory was still there.

It was.

He made a few meals. Small things. Just to show May that he was trying. Just to show her that he wasn't checking out.

He feared that he was turning her into his caregiver. She wasn't there yet, but the fear lingered. Is it only a matter of time?

But then he realized something. All the struggles. All the obstacles. The abuse. The war. The betrayal. The crash.

They hadn't broken him. They had trained him.

He was not "recovered." He was still in a state of "To Be Continued."

But as he hit Submit on the VA claim, staring at the evidence of his own survival, he realized that the victory wasn't in the approval letter that might come months from now.

The victory was that he fought back.

EPILOGUE
THE ANCHOR

Today - North Texas

I sit on the couch.

It is the same spot where I spent countless hours as "The Shell," staring blankly at a TV screen, controller in hand, building digital fortresses in *Minecraft* to keep the monsters out.

But today, the controller is gone. In my lap sits a laptop. I am not building a wall anymore; I am building a bridge.

The house is quiet, but it isn't silent. It is alive. My youngest son is napping, exhausted from a morning of chaos. My oldest is on the floor, engrossed in a tablet.

I look across the room at May. She is tirelessly hand-knitting a custom blanket, her fingers moving in a blur. She looks tired, but there is a rhythm to her movement that speaks of peace, not panic.

I look back at the screen. I know I am not the perfect father. I have the "Best Dad Ever" t-shirt, but I know the title is a goal, not a trophy.

I used to believe that the "American Dream" was the house, the job, and the lawn. I thought it was a destination you reached after you checked all the boxes.

I know better now. The fairy tale doesn't exist. But what *does* exist is the blood, sweat, and tears each and every one of us puts into this life together.

We are all human. We all fall short. Whether we hurt each other or just made devastating mistakes in our past, we have all been the villain in someone's story.

It is up to us to choose to wake up every day and say to ourselves, "Today, I choose to be the hero of my story."

That is what I am learning to do. Every day, one act at a time, one choice at a time.

Find a way to put a smile on May's face, or goof around in a way that will make my boys laugh.

I tell myself.

And for the first time, I am choosing to do the things that *I* need.

I am not serving my country. I am not serving my state. I have no debt to be paid for the opportunities I busted my ass to achieve. I am serving myself.

I am allowing myself grace.

Sometimes that looks like choosing to build a Lego set by myself instead of with my son because I need the quiet focus. Sometimes it's saying I need a nap instead of helping May with the dishes because my battery is blinking red.

These are no longer options for me; these are the prescriptions I need so I am able to give my all to those I love.

It is no different than putting the oxygen mask on in an airliner. You put it on yourself first so that you can then assist others.

I have learned that I owe my loved ones the best of me, and the only way to give them my best is for me to invest in myself.

And to you - the reader, the veteran, the weary traveler holding this book - I want to leave you with one simple truth.

The world will tell a person who is neuro-divergent or physio-divergent that they are "less than." They will tell someone who has survived trauma that they are somehow broken by their circumstances. They tell those who battle mental health issues that they are not fit enough to participate in all that life has to offer.

I am here to tell you to shut that noise out. Those who tell you that you *can't* need to shove their judgment where the sun doesn't shine.

You, by definition, have adapted and overcome. You navigated a world that was not built to accommodate you, and you found a way. Your strength has gotten you this far; do not let the naysayers take your victory away from you.

It is easy to be "typical" in this world. It takes a Goliath to be divergent.

Puff out your chest. Be proud of who you are. Wear your divergence on your sleeve, end the stigma, and proudly say, "I am different, I struggle, but I am strong, and I am a champion."

This isn't a mantra to make you believe; this is a fact. You have pushed through all the bullshit, and you are still here.

Yes, it is exhausting at times. Yes, there are times you must stop and just take a break. There is absolutely nothing wrong with that, because in the end, you are the only one who dictates what it takes to put one foot in front of the other.

You are the author of your story.

And I am here to tell you one simple truth.

Your Story Matters.

About the Author

Andrew Rose is a combat veteran of Operation Iraqi Freedom and a survivor of the unforgiving streets of the Bronx. Born into a world defined by poverty and a volatile household, he learned early on to navigate the line between predator and prey. After 9/11, he traded one war zone for another, deploying to Balad as an infantryman where he survived the chaos of the Sunni Triangle and the invisible wounds of a Traumatic Brain Injury.

Today, Rose is an entrepreneur, a dedicated father, and a fierce advocate for veterans navigating the silent battles of transition. *Between Two Worlds* is his debut memoir, chronicling his journey from the "Charity Kid" to the "Warrior," and finally to a man learning that his greatest strength lies in his divergence.